Books by the same author:

THE WIZARD IN THE WOODS

Jean Ure

Illustrations by
David Anstey

CANDLEWICK PRESS
CAMBRIDGE, MASSACHUSETTS

First U.S. edition 1992
First published in Great Britain in 1990 by
Walker Books Ltd., London.

Library of Congress Cataloging-in-Publication Data

Ure, Jean.   The wizard in the woods/by Jean Ure;
illustrations by David Anstey.
Summary: Ben-Muzzy, a second class junior wizard,
bungles a spell during his Junior Wizard exams and
ends up in Penny Woods where he meets Joel
and Gemma and their adventures begin.
[1. Wizards—Fiction.   2. Magic—Fiction.]
I. Anstey, David, ill.   II. Title.
P27.U64Wj   1992   [Fic]dc20   91-58770
ISBN 1-56402-110-6

10 9 8 7 6 5 4 3 2 1

Printed in the U.S.A.

Candlewick Press
2067 Massachusetts Avenue
Cambridge, Massachusetts 02140

To Julia and Laura,
who read this book before anyone else

Chapter One

Ben-Muzzy caught his breath in excitement and pulled his yellow cloak tightly around him as he stood at the foot of the steps and gazed up at the large building in front of him. There was a sign over the front door that said:

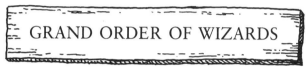

GRAND ORDER OF WIZARDS

Each letter was made up of thousands of colored stars, all winking and blinking and flashing.

Ben-Muzzy had been inside the building only once before. That was when he had taken his very first examination in simple magic and had been enrolled as a second-class junior wizard. He had been given a yellow cloak and a tall black hat like a church steeple and a book of easy spells, and he had taken his wizard's oath: "I promise to be a good wizard, to honor and obey the Wizard of all the Wizards, and to do my best to help people. I will cast no spells except good spells, and I will not meddle with black magic."

That had been a whole year ago. Since then Ben-Muzzy had been studying very hard and working for a Grand High Wizard called Wollibar. Wollibar had a first-class junior wizard working for him as well. The first-class junior was called Podnock. He thought himself superior and tended to boss Ben-Muzzy around. It was always Podnock who bagged all the really interesting tasks such as stirring the magic cauldron or feeding the black cat. (Ben-Muzzy was not allowed anywhere near the black cat. Black cats are temperamental animals, quite capable of quitting their spells for days on end and simply sitting sulking.)

What Ben-Muzzy's work mainly consisted of was collecting owls' feathers and four-leafed clovers for Wollibar's spells, or cleaning the magic cauldron, or polishing the magic wand. He enjoyed doing these things, but he did sometimes grow a little impatient.

"Always the same with you young wizards," grumbled Wollibar. "Always wanting to magic before you can spell."

One day, quite by accident, Ben-Muzzy had changed Podnock into a black beetle and been unable to change him back again. Wollibar had been very angry indeed (and so had Podnock, afterward). It had taken him and two other Grand High Wizards several hours to change Podnock back from a black beetle to a junior wizard. They had had to use six tons of acorns and form a magic circle with three black cats in the center, and Wollibar had burned a hole in his new cauldron. After that, Ben-Muzzy had been told he must practice no spells on other people unless he was under supervision. Podnock said that if he wanted to change *himself* into a black beetle or a bunch of tadpoles he was welcome to do so, but there would be trouble if he changed Podnock into anything else.

"Even if it's something nice, like a molasses cookie. I'm working very hard," said Podnock, "and I don't have the time to waste being changed into things. Just go away quietly by yourself and practice white rabbits."

"White rabbits are too easy," complained Ben-

Muzzy. "Anyone can produce rabbits from top hats."

"You can't!" retorted Podnock. "I was watching you the other day, and one of yours had bright blue whiskers."

"It was supposed to," said Ben-Muzzy; but Podnock only jeered and said, "Rabbit with blue whiskers!"

"If you want to grow up to be a senior wizard," said Wollibar sternly, "you'll have to be a little more careful than that."

Today Ben-Muzzy was going to take extra special care, because today was the day when second-class junior wizards all over the land had to take their exams. If they passed them, they became first-class junior wizards, which was what Ben-Muzzy wanted more than anything in the world. Being a first-class wizard meant you could wear a beautiful bright green cloak, like Podnock, instead of this horrible yellow thing that showed everyone immediately that you were still only a beginner.

A puff of smoke appeared at Ben-Muzzy's side, and a senior wizard stepped out of it.

"What's this?" said the senior wizard.

"Examination day?"

Ben-Muzzy nodded shyly.

"Scared?" asked the senior wizard.

"A little," said Ben-Muzzy.

The senior wizard laughed. "Nothing to be scared of! Just think before you spell. Best of luck, young wizard!" Then he folded his cloak around him, nodded his head, and flew carelessly off, up the flight of steps and in through the front door.

Ben-Muzzy gazed after him enviously. He wondered how it felt to be able to fly like that, with your feet never touching the ground. He remembered once reading how to do it in one of Wollibar's books. It had sounded pretty simple. Something like . . . "Gordee ublin ubble." Or was it "ublee gordin gubble"? or "gublee ordin—"

Ben-Muzzy had no chance to wonder what else it might have been. With a great *whoosh!* he found himself rising into the air, being propelled like a rocket, up the steps toward the door. The door, fortunately, was open. Ben-Muzzy shot through it and into the entrance hall. A sign saying:

flashed past his right ear; a row of gape-mouthed juniors stood watching from the foot of some stairs. Ben-Muzzy attempted an airy wave and bounced, painfully, off a wall.

He was going at a simply tremendous speed, far faster than the senior wizard. He would be arrested for dangerous flying if he weren't careful. Ben-Muzzy flapped his arms, trying to brake: nothing happened. He suddenly realized . . . he didn't know how to stop!

"Help!" bleated Ben-Muzzy. "I don't know how to stop!"

A very old and wise-looking Grand High Wizard was walking down the corridor, a black cat perched on his shoulder.

"Help!" cried Ben-Muzzy.

His yellow cloak billowed out and caught the Grand High Wizard's hat in its folds. Ben-Muzzy carried the hat along with him. The black cat spat and leapt after him.

"Help me!" shrieked Ben-Muzzy again. "I'm out of control!"

There was an open window ahead of him. He would go flying straight through it and out over the rooftops. He might go on flying forever.

"He-e-e-e-e-elp!" screamed Ben-Muzzy, at the top of his voice.

The Grand High Wizard sighed.

"Elbbu nilbu eedrog," he said calmly.

Ben-Muzzy sat down on the floor with a bump. The cat caught up with him and stood spitting. Ben-Muzzy scrambled shakily to his feet and found that he had been sitting on the Grand High Wizard's hat. It was crushed.

"Is that my hat?" said the Grand High Wizard, glaring. "What a shocking business! That hat was new only last week. You young wizards really ought to be more careful."

"I'm spellfully sorry," stammered Ben-Muzzy. "If you know a spell that will un-crush it again, I'll s-say it for you."

"Thank you," said the Grand High Wizard coldly. "I prefer to say my own spells." He picked up the black cat and set it on his shoulder. "If I were you," he said, "I would stick to white rabbits in the future. Leave the more complicated business to your elders and betters."

Ben-Muzzy turned bright pink with shame. What a dreadful thing to have happened! He had knocked off a Grand High Wizard's hat (a new hat), he had sat on the hat, he had crushed the hat, and he had probably upset the black cat so much that it would refuse to help with any spells for weeks to come. He was lucky the Grand High Wizard hadn't taken him to the Magic Court for punishment.

Crestfallen, Ben-Muzzy crept around the corridors in search of the examination room. On the way he passed another second-class junior, proudly carrying a new green cloak over his arm. In half an hour, if only he could manage to do all his spells correctly, he too would be carrying a new green cloak. The thought cheered him up and made him feel a little braver. Briskly he stepped out down the passage until he came to a notice that said:

JUNIOR EXAMINATIONS IN HERE

The door opened by itself as Ben-Muzzy approached. Inside the room sat a Master Wizard, wearing spectacles and a white beard.

"Second-class wizard Ben-Muzzy?" he said. "You're five minutes late. Wizards should never be late."

Ben-Muzzy grew hot and red. "I lost my way," he mumbled.

"Lost your way?" The Master Wizard raised his eyebrows. "How could you possibly lose your way? There's a large signpost in the front hall."

Ben-Muzzy wondered whether or not he should explain that he had flown through the front hall so fast that he had not had time to notice any signposts, but before he could make up his mind, the Master Wizard had pulled out a list of questions.

"Now then," he said, "take a seat, Ben-Muzzy, and we shall see how much you know. First question: Which way does a magic circle move, to the left or to the right?"

"That depends on what sort of spell it is," said Ben-Muzzy. He knew all about magic circles. "If it's a spell for doing things, then the circle moves to the left. But if it's a spell for undoing things, the circle moves to the right."

"Quite correct. Can you give me an example of a spell that undoes something?"

Ben-Muzzy thought for a moment.

"Yes," he said. "If you sat on someone's hat and crushed it and you wanted to get it back into the right sort of shape again, that would be an undoing sort of spell."

"Excellent!" said the Master. "Most imaginative! I shall give you full points."

The questions went on for another ten minutes. There were twenty of them in all, and Ben-Muzzy knew the answers to eighteen. He felt pretty pleased with himself. Then the Master said that it was "Time for some practical work," and immediately Ben-Muzzy's insides began trying to tie themselves in knots. He really must remember all his spells correctly and not make stupid mistakes! It would be too dreadful if he produced rabbits with blue whiskers, and worse still if he turned the master into a black beetle.

"Don't look so worried!" said the Master. "I'm not going to ask you to go flying, or anything like that."

At the word "flying," Ben-Muzzy's insides promptly tied themselves in a tight knot.

"OK," said the Master. "White rabbits . . ."

In the next few minutes Ben-Muzzy succeeded in producing two rabbits from a hat (one was admittedly a little cross-eyed, but at least neither of them had blue whiskers); he grew a fine big sunflower from a daffodil bulb (it was a pink sunflower, but the Master didn't seem to mind); and he made a list of names on a blackboard disappear all by themselves and come back again in roughly the right order.

After that, the spells became more difficult.

"The next thing I want you to do," said the Master, "is something that most junior wizards seem to find amusing. I expect you've already practiced a little by yourself. I just want you to make yourself invisible, walk across the room and open the window, come back and sit down, and then reappear. Can you do that, do you think?"

Ben-Muzzy nodded happily. He was full of confidence now that he had managed to produce two white rabbits without a blue whisker between them. Why, he knew the spell for becoming invisible so well he could say it backward!

Unfortunately, he did say it backward . . .

Before his eyes, the Master began to disappear. First his hands and feet, then his body, finally his face, until there was nothing left but his clothes. Ben-Muzzy watched, pink and horrified, as the clothes also faded into nothingness.

There was a long silence, and then the Master spoke: "You seem to have made a slight mistake," he said.

Ben-Muzzy tried to say that he was sorry, but no sound would come from his mouth. He just sat and gaped at the space on the other side of the Master's desk, where the Master was sitting invisible.

"If by any chance," suggested the Master, "you know the spell that will bring me back again, I shall consider giving you half the points."

Ben-Muzzy squeezed his brain until it hurt.

"Offl—" he said.

"Go on," said the Master.

"Oofl flin doola!" gasped Ben-Muzzy.

Slowly the Master began to reappear, starting with his hands and his feet, then his body and then his face, until at last he was all there again. Only one thing was missing: "What about my clothes?" demanded the Master in an awful voice.

Ben-Muzzy grew pinker than ever.

"You young wizards!" said the Master. Impatiently he made some magic passes in the air and reclothed himself. "You really must learn to concentrate."

There was only one spell left now. Ben-Muzzy sat forward in his chair, concentrating hard.

"This time," said the Master, "I want you to

magic yourself up to Room 3 on the ground floor. My assistant is there waiting for you. He will bring you back here again and tell me whether you arrived according to the rules, and all in one piece."

This was a very difficult spell indeed. Some of the hardest spells in the land were those of removing yourself from one place to another. Really top wizards like Wollibar could magic themselves wherever they wanted, but even senior wizards sometimes left part of themselves behind and had to go back for it. And junior wizards often ended up in the wrong place altogether.

"Take your time," urged the Master. "And for magic's sake, if you don't know the correct spell just say so."

Ben-Muzzy was almost sure that he knew it.

He stood up and pulled his cloak around him, swallowed three times, and frowned nervously.

"Kloo kloh klaw
Klay klay klee,
Number three
Let it be!"

The Master gasped and leaped from his chair, but he was too late: Ben-Muzzy, in a flash of blue light, had disappeared.

"Bless my magic buttons!" said the Master. "Rabbit droppings and horse hair! Wherever has he gone?"

They searched the entire building for him, but he was nowhere to be found. All the grandest High Wizards from all over the land, were called to an urgent conference, but there was nothing they could do about it.

Ben-Muzzy had vanished, and no one knew where.

Chapter Two

Ben-Muzzy picked himself up and stared around in dismay. What had happened to him? One minute he had been standing in front of the Master Wizard, the next he was sitting on the ground in a place that he had never seen before.

He seemed to be in the middle of a thick forest. All around him were trees, tall and dark and gloomy. In the distance he could hear the ripple of water, and from somewhere nearby the sound of a woodpecker noisily drilling holes in a rotted tree stump.

"Where am I?" wailed Ben-Muzzy.

Nobody answered, except the woodpecker.

"Tee hee hee!" shrilled the woodpecker, clinging to its stump.

"Gaargh," added a crow from a nearby branch.

Ben-Muzzy took a few steps in one direction, then a few steps in another. Then he stopped and called, "Hello? Is anybody there?"

"Only me!" cackled the woodpecker, preparing to start drilling again.

"And me," said the crow.

Ben-Muzzy stood very still and sniffed at the air. There was something about it that was not quite right; something that made his hair prickle beneath his hat. It didn't smell bad, but it certainly didn't smell like home.

A terrible and terrifying thought suddenly came to him. Was it possible that he, second-class junior wizard Ben-Muzzy, had accidentally stumbled on a piece of magic so powerful that it had transported him to another land? He knew that there was such magic, for Grand High Wizards like Wollibar used it all the time. The difference was that Grand High Wizards used it on purpose and Ben-Muzzy had used it by mistake. And Ben-Muzzy wasn't at all sure that he knew the correct spell for taking himself back again. Obviously there were spells for taking you back; in fact he had seen them in one of Wollibar's books. But even if he could manage to remember any, what use would they be? All the really big important spells he had ever read about needed three people to form a magic circle, and where was he going to find any people in this strange land?

Ben-Muzzy sank onto a patch of moss at the foot of a tree and burst loudly into tears. He was lonely and frightened, and he didn't know where he was. The woodpecker looked across at him angrily and flapped his wings. Such a disturbance in the middle of meal time!

"Gaaargh!" said the crow.

Ben-Muzzy just went on crying.

Joel and Gemma were walking through the woods on their way home from school. They were arguing. They often argued.

"I want a sheepdog," Gemma was saying. "An Old English sheepdog, like in *Peter Pan*."

"Sooner have a dalmatian," said Joel.

"I don't want a dalmatian, I want a sheepdog."

"If we had a dalmatian we could call it Spot."

"If we had a sheepdog we could call her Flossie."

Joel drew a deep breath and slashed with his hand at a clump of ferns. He and Gemma were twins. They looked very alike with their dark curly hair and brown eyes, but that didn't keep them from quarreling.

"Why don't we have *two* dogs?"

"Cause they wouldn't let us."

"They might, if we asked."

Joel said, "Humph!" He didn't sound very hopeful. "Let's go and see if there are any fish in the stream."

A boy at school had told him he had seen a whale in it the other day. That was nonsense, of course; you didn't get whales in streams. Still he must have seen something.

"You know Graham Roberts?" he said. "He told—"

"Sh!" Gemma had suddenly stopped, her head tilted to one side. "What's that?"

Joel also stopped. He also tilted his head to one side.

"Sounds like someone crying," said Gemma.

Gemma was right. It did sound like someone crying.

"Come on!" cried Joel. "Let's go and see!"

Joel charged off and was followed closely by Gemma. They reached a clearing and stopped in amazement. Crouched under an oak tree, sobbing as if his heart would break, was the strangest little being wrapped in a yellow cloak. On his head was a tall black hat. On his feet, which could just be seen poking from under his cloak, he had a pair of bright red slippers with curly toes.

For a moment the twins were too surprised to say anything. Gemma, as usual, was the first to recover.

"Must be in costume," she whispered.

"Could be a man from Mars."

The woodpecker, at this, gave a loud shriek of laughter. Ben-Muzzy stopped crying and looked up. His eyes widened and he stared very hard at the twins as if he had never seen anything like them before. Gemma stepped forward.

"Do you mind not staring at us like that?" she said. She said it very politely. "We don't like people staring at us just because we're twins."

"Twins?" said Ben-Muzzy.

"Almost identical but not quite," Joel told him. "And I'm five minutes older than she is."

"And we think it's very bad manners to stare," added Gemma. "We can't help being twins. We didn't ask to be twins. We just are."

"I beg your pardon," said Ben-Muzzy humbly. "I didn't realize."

"That's all right," said Gemma. "What are you crying for, anyway? Have you lost something?"

"Or are you a man from Mars?"

Ben-Muzzy shook his head. Tears came into his eyes, and he wiped them away with a corner of his cloak.

"I'm a wizard," he said.

Joel and Gemma looked at each other.

"You mean you're dressed as a wizard," said Gemma. To Joel she added, "I told you he was in costume."

"Were you going to a party?"

"I was taking my exam," said Ben-Muzzy. "Only I said the wrong spell and now I'm l-lost, and I don't know how to g-get myself back!"

"We'll help you," said Gemma. "And try to stop crying. You'll give yourself the most awful headache."

"But I'm l-lost!" wept Ben-Muzzy.

"You can't be *very* lost," said Joel. Three Penny Woods were only small woods; not at all the sort of woods that people got lost in.

"But I d-don't know w-where I am!"

"You're in Three Penny Woods. And if you go in that direction," Joel pointed straight ahead, "you'll get to Tanners Lane, and if you go in the other direction," he pointed back along the path, the way that he and Gemma had come, "you'll get to the main road."

Ben-Muzzy received this information in silence. It was good to know where he was, but it didn't really help him.

"Where have you come from?" said Gemma.

Ben-Muzzy picked up a corner of his cloak and blotted at his eyes. "I've come from the Land of Wizards."

There was a pause. This time, the twins avoided looking at each other.

"Where exactly would that be?" said Gemma.

"I don't know!" Ben Muzzy's tears burst forth again. "If I knew where it was I might be able to get back there!"

The twins waited a moment in embarrassed silence as Ben-Muzzy wept into the corner of his cloak. Suddenly, very loudly, Joel spoke.

"There are no such thing as wizards," he said.

"Yes, there are!" Ben-Muzzy blotted his nose fiercely. "I'm a wizard. A second-class junior wizard, only I s-said the wrong sp-ell and now I'm l-lost!"

Joel pursed his lips. Whales in the stream were one thing; wizards in the woods were another. Wizards in the woods were ridiculous.

Gemma, squatting down by Ben-Muzzy, took out her handkerchief and offered it to him. "Would you like to borrow this?" she said.

Ben-Muzzy looked at it doubtfully.

"I've only used it once," said Gemma. "And it's better than messing up your nice cloak. Specially as you're going to a party."

Ben-Muzzy snatched at the handkerchief. "I'm not g-going to a party! I said the wrong sp-pell and it all w-went wrong!"

"So why don't you just say another spell," said Joel, "and make it go right?"

Ben-Muzzy blew his nose on Gemma's handkerchief. "I would if I knew one, but I can't remember them right!"

"I'm sure you could if you tried." Joel said it sternly, like Miss Heryot at school. "It's a question of applying yourself."

Ben-Muzzy sniffed miserably into the handkerchief.

"I'd need a magic circle," he said. "Where would I get a magic circle from?" He looked at the twins and for the first time a small flicker of hope appeared in his eyes. "I don't suppose you'd like to be one?" he said.

Gemma beamed. "Of course we would! We'd love to."

Joel was more cautious. After all, it was

nearly dinner time. "What exactly is a magic circle?" he said.

"What is a magic circle?" Ben-Muzzy was shocked. He had thought everyone knew about magic circles. Didn't these twin-people go to school? "It's three people holding hands while one of them says a spell."

"That sounds like a nice game," said Gemma.

Joel privately thought it sounded sort of silly. Sort of *childish*.

"Of course you really need three black cats," said Ben-Muzzy. "Three black cats or a magic cauldron to stand in the middle."

Gemma looked grave. "I'm afraid we don't have any of those. We might be able to borrow a saucepan. Would a saucepan do?"

"Not unless it was magic," said Ben-Muzzy. Really these people didn't know anything. A saucepan was a saucepan: a cauldron was a cauldron.

"Oh, dear," said Gemma.

"It's all right, there are ways to get around it . . . in an emergency, substitute three oak trees."

"Oh, well! We've got plenty of those."

"They're a little old-fashioned, of course. No

one uses them very much these days, but they did in my grandfather's time. My grandfather," said Ben-Muzzy, unable to resist the temptation to do a little showing off, "was a Grand High."

"Ours is a doctor," said Gemma. "He works in a hospital. So does our dad. Our d—"

"Never mind all that!" said Joel. "Let's talk about this magic circle thing. What's supposed to happen when you've said the spell?"

"Well, if it works right," said Ben-Muzzy, "if I've remembered it right, we'll be back home before you can say abracadabra."

"You'll be back home," Joel said. "But where will we be?" It was all nonsense, of course; wizards and spells and abracadabra. He wasn't pretending he believed any of it. "Do we stay here or do we go with you?"

"Oh, you'd come with me." Ben-Muzzy said it quite happily. "But there's no need to worry. Wollibar could get you back easily enough. He knows all kinds of spells."

"Who's Wollibar?"

"He's the Grand High that I work for. It wouldn't take him two shakes of a gnat's tail to send you back."

"Of course, we have only your word for that," said Joel. It sounded sort of risky to him. Which was to say, it *would* sound sort of risky, if there was any truth to it, which of course there wasn't. On the other hand . . .

Somewhere in the distance, a church struck the hour: that made up Joel's mind. "Look here," he said, "we can't make magic circles just now; we've got to get home for dinner. Maybe tomorrow."

Ben-Muzzy's face began to crumple.

"All right?" Joel threw his school bag over his shoulder. "We'll let you know."

"We really do have to be going now," said Gemma. "Our mother will be starting to worry. I expect," she added, "that yours will, too. Why don't you go home and have dinner, and we'll play magic circles in the morning? It's Saturday tomorrow. We could play all day if you wanted."

As the twins moved off, Ben-Muzzy made one last desperate plea: "I could make you two white rabbits out of a top hat!"

"Sorry," said Joel. "Don't want two white rabbits."

Ben-Muzzy's face fell. He stood miserably in the clearing, twisting Gemma's handkerchief around one of his fingers.

"I tell you what," said Gemma. She turned. "You couldn't make us a dog out of a top hat?"

"A dog?" Ben-Muzzy put his fingers to his mouth and chewed nervously on the handkerchief. He wasn't too sure about dogs. He supposed it could be done, although as far as he knew no one ever did produce dogs from top hats. After all, what would be the point of it?

"Well," he said, slowly, "I could try."

"A big shaggy dog with hair all over its eyes?" said Gemma.

"A white dog," said Joel, "with spots?"

"You keep out of it," said Gemma. "It was my idea, not yours!"

Ben-Muzzy held up a hand. "You're confusing me," he said. "Just wait a minute and I'll see what I can do."

He stood up, wrapped his cloak around him and walked to the center of the clearing.

"Obbledy obbledy dubbledy gook!" he said.

Immediately, a shiny black top hat appeared in his hand.

"So he *is* a wizard," said Joel. "How extraordinary!"

"Sh!" said Gemma. "You're interrupting the spell."

Ben-Muzzy made a few magic passes over the hat. "Fillivan fullivan upwigo!"

The hat flew into the air. Clouds of smoke filled the clearing. When the smoke faded, the twins could see Ben-Muzzy standing proudly by the side of a large pink animal with blue spots

and flapping ears and a long pink trunk.

"There!" he said. "Your dog!"

"That's not a dog," said Joel. "That's a baby elephant. A pink baby elephant with blue spots on it."

"Oh." Ben-Muzzy's proud smile faded. "I thought it was a dog."

"Well, it's not," said Joel. "It's an elephant."

Gemma suddenly went racing across the clearing. She threw her arms around the strange

pink animal and planted a fond kiss on the end of its trunk. "Who cares? It's the most beautiful elephant—so pretty! What a clever thing to do! Producing an elephant—out of a hat! You wouldn't think that an elephant would fit in a hat!"

Ben-Muzzy beamed at her gratefully. "So will it be all right? Instead of a dog?"

"We-e-ell . . ."

Gemma looked at Joel. Joel looked at the elephant.

"Well, I wouldn't mind keeping an elephant," he said. "But I don't know what our parents will say. The trouble with elephants is, they eat such a lot."

Ben-Muzzy nodded sadly. An air of deep dejection hung over him.

"We could always ask," said Gemma.

"Let's all go home and take the elephant with us and see what they say."

"Me too?" asked Ben-Muzzy, cheering up.

"All of us," said Gemma. She tugged at one of the elephant's ears. "Come along, Flossie!"

"Spot!" snapped Joel.

"Flossie!" snapped Gemma.

"Spot!" snapped Joel.

"Flossie," said Gemma. "And that reminds me
. . ." She turned to Ben-Muzzy. "We don't know
what your name is."

"It's Ben-Muzzy," said Ben-Muzzy.

"What a very nice name," said Gemma. "I'm
Gemma and this is my brother Joel. And this is
our elephant, Flossie."

"Spot!"

"Flossie!"

They started off through the woods together,
Joel and Gemma and Ben-Muzzy, with the pink
and blue elephant ambling along in their wake.

Chapter Three

They left Ben-Muzzy in the greenhouse.

"You'll be nice and warm in here," said Gemma. "If we took you indoors, they'd only start asking questions."

"Besides," added Joel, "we've got our gran staying with us. She might be scared if she saw a wizard."

"I understand," said Ben-Muzzy humbly.

"We won't forget you," Gemma assured him. "We'll save some of our dinner and bring it out to you before we go to bed. What sort of things do wizards like to eat?"

"Just about everything," said Ben-Muzzy hopefully.

"Do they like sandwiches and bread-and-jam and chocolate cake?"

"Yes," said Ben-Muzzy. "They like all of that." He wasn't sure what it was, but it sounded good.

"OK," said Joel. "We'll see what we can do. We're going to go and put the elephant away now."

They had decided not to show the elephant to their parents right away. In their experience grown-ups needed time to get used to things. As Joel had said, an elephant might come as a bit of a shock. They were a little doubtful about where to keep it in the meantime.

"We can't leave it in the garage," said Gemma, "in case it sits on the car."

"And anyway, Dad would see it when he got back."

At the moment the elephant was standing in the lane, outside the back gate, with its trunk hanging over the fence.

"Do you suppose," said Gemma, "that it would go in the shed?"

They opened the gate and the elephant obligingly squeezed itself through the narrow opening. There wasn't much room for it in the shed, but at least it could sit down or stand or turn in a circle.

"It's only for tonight," said Gemma. "And we can bring it some rolls after dinner."

Joel was thoughtful on his way up to the house. "If we're going to feed elephants *and* wizards," he said, "it's not going to leave very much for us, is it?"

Dinner was already on the table—Joel was relieved to note that there was a lot of it.

"You're late," said their mother. "I thought I told you to come straight home?"

"We were looking for whales in the stream," said Joel. He helped himself to a handful of bread and reached out for the butter.

"Whales," said his grandmother, "live in the sea, not in streams. I should have thought a boy your age would know that."

"People *say* they don't live in streams," said Gemma. "Like people *say* there aren't such things as fairies. *Or* wizards," she added, spreading four slices of bread and butter very thickly with jam. "But there might be."

The twins' mother was frowning at their heaped-up plates. "Are you really going to eat all that?" she said.

"I'm really hungry," said Joel. He slipped three of the slices of bread and butter onto his lap, folded them in half, and worked them around, one by one, to the back pocket of his jeans. "You know this dog?" he said. "This dog you said we could have for our birthday? If we decided we'd rather have some other kind of animal, would that be all right?"

"Why?" said his mother, automatically suspicious. "What other kind of animal did you have in mind?"

"Elephants," said Gemma.

"Well, of course, if you're going to be silly—Gemma, I do wish you wouldn't bolt your food like that! You had four slices of bread and jam on that plate a second ago"

"I'm a very fast eater," said Gemma. "May I have some chocolate cake?"

Joel reached out for some more bread. "What if we happened to find one?" he said.

"Find what?"

"An elephant."

"Then it would go straight to the zoo."

"Even if it was only a small elephant?"

"Whatever size elephant it was."

"But why?" said Gemma, wondering if Ben-Muzzy would object to eating bread-and-jam and chocolate cake all mixed up together.

"Because small elephants grow into big elephants and eat far too much . . . just as you are!" The twins' mother snatched up the plate of chocolate cake as Gemma's hand closed over another slice. "You'll make yourself sick!"

"I'm hungry," said Gemma.

Her grandmother sniffed. "When I was young," she said, "we were never allowed more than one slice of cake for dessert."

Next morning while the twins were still in bed, a most terrible scream rang through the house. They rushed out at once onto the landing, struggling into their jeans and sweaters. The door of their grandmother's room was open. Their father was hovering at the entrance; their mother was inside.

"What's the matter with her, what's the matter with her?" their father was saying irritably.

"She says she saw a pink elephant in the garden."

"Pink elephant?"

"That's what she says . . . a pink elephant with blue spots."

"Acid indigestion!" snapped the twins' father.

The twins giggled nervously. Their father turned on them. "Don't you two start! You can come downstairs with me and help get the breakfast while your mother looks after your gran."

Meekly, the twins followed their father downstairs.

"How did it get out?" whispered Gemma.

"Don't ask me," said Joel. "I suppose you didn't lock the door."

"*I* didn't shut the door," said Gemma, "you did. Or didn't," she added, "as the case may be."

Joel opened his mouth. "I d—"

He was interrupted by an angry roaring. "Who's been playing in my rose bed?" roared the twins' father.

Dropping the kettle, which he had been filling at the sink, he tore open the back door and raced out. Full of foreboding, the twins crept after him. The garden was in a state of fearsome confusion. The roses had been trampled on, the grass had been rolled on, a fence had been knocked down and all the heads had disappeared from their mother's prize dahlias.

"It must have been hungry," suggested Gemma.

Their father strode down the path toward the back gate. The twins stood undecided in the middle of the mud patch that had once been a smooth lawn.

"Pst! Pst!" Ben-Muzzy was beckoning to them from behind the gate. Keeping one eye on their father, they sidled over to him.

"It got out," whispered Ben-Muzzy. "It got out and ate up all those flower things before I could stop it, and then it started playing games all by itself in the middle of the grass. I tried to get it back, but it wouldn't come."

"So where is it now?"said Joel.

"Well—" Ben-Muzzy blushed. "I tried to turn it into a dog for you, only something went

wrong with the spell and,"—he drew out a hand from behind his back—"it turned into this, instead."

A small white mouse stared up at them with beady eyes. It twitched its nostrils, then licked a tiny paw and began cleaning behind its ears.

"I hope you don't mind," said Ben-Muzzy.

The twins heaved a sigh of relief.

"It's probably happier as a mouse," said Gemma.

"That's what I thought," agreed Ben-Muzzy. He set it down carefully on the ground. "I can always make you a dog when we get back home."

"Watch out. Dad's coming back," said Joel. "You wait there, Ben-Muzzy, and we'll meet you after breakfast."

The twins' parents were very angry indeed at

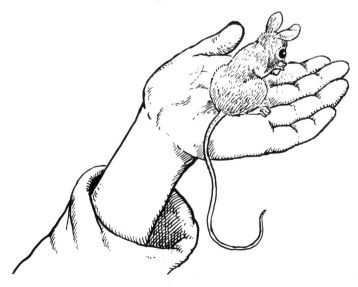

the state of their back garden. They strongly suspected that the twins were at the bottom of things—the twins usually were at the bottom of things—but, as their mother said, "I don't see how even the twins could have gotten hold of a pink elephant."

After breakfast, they asked if they could take a picnic lunch to the woods and stay out until dinner time.

"I suppose so," said their mother. "But you must promise to be back by half-past five and not to speak to any strangers."

That was all right: Ben-Muzzy wasn't a stranger. He might have been yesterday, but he wasn't today.

"Could we have a really *big* lunch?" said Joel. "A *really* big lunch, with sandwiches and things?"

Their mother filled up their knapsacks with food. They had cheese sandwiches and potato chips and more chocolate cake and granola bars and two bananas and an enormous bottle of juice.

"Where do they put it all?" said their grandmother.

The twins took their knapsacks, collected Ben-Muzzy from the garden, crossed the lane, and went into the woods.

"So where should we do the magic circle?" said Joel.

Ben-Muzzy looked pointedly at the knapsacks. "Before wizards can do spells," he said, "they have to have their breakfast. Breakfast is very important to wizards."

"How awful!" said Gemma. "I was forgetting you hadn't eaten. What would you like? Cheese sandwich? Potato chips? Chocolate cake?"

"Yes, please," said Ben-Muzzy, eagerly.

He ate a little bit of everything and drank some juice, and then they walked farther into the woods, looking for three oak trees. Ben-Muzzy said that the three oak trees had to grow close together, so that they could form the magic circle inside them.

"Cats and cauldrons inside," he said. "Oak trees outside."

Fortunately the woods were full of oak trees. They soon found three that Ben-Muzzy said would be all right.

"But I've got to remember the spell first. It's

no use forming a magic circle if you don't know what spell you're going to use."

Ben-Muzzy had spent all night in the greenhouse thinking about spells. He had dreamed about spells and he had had nightmares about spells. In one of Wollibar's books, "Magic for Coming and Going," there had been long lists of them—spells of transportation, they had been called. Ben-Muzzy had learned several by heart. The only trouble was that in spite of learning them by heart he couldn't always remember exactly where it was they transported you to . . .

All he could do was hope for the best. If the first spell took them to the wrong place, he would just have to wait for his magic to come back and then try another one. If at first you don't succeed, then spell, spell again; that was what Wollibar said.

Ben-Muzzy cleared his throat. "Very well," he said, "if you're ready."

"We're ready," said Joel. "We're waiting for you. I hope you've got the spell right; we don't want any mistakes."

Ben-Muzzy flapped his cloak in a careless

gesture. "I have been apprenticed," he said, "to the highest in the land."

"Didn't keep you from getting lost!" retorted Joel.

Gemma jabbed her twin in the ribs. "Stop being so mean!"

They joined hands and Ben-Muzzy told the twins to close their eyes very tightly and concentrate. He felt a little bit apprehensive, but very proud and self-important. Why, this was almost like being a grand high!

For an awful moment he couldn't decide whether a spell-for-taking-you-back was a doing or an undoing sort of spell, and whether the circle should move to the left or to the right, but at last he decided it was probably a straightforward doing spell, because after all it wasn't exactly the same thing as turning Podnock into a black beetle and then turning him back into Podnock again.

"Six steps to the left, six steps to the right," chanted Ben-Muzzy, "then all the way around. Are you ready?"

They took six steps to the left, they took six steps to the right. Ben-Muzzy began his spell:

"Wishalong wosholong takalong backalong. Upwigo downwigo—"

A vivid blue light appeared. For a second or so it hovered uncertainly over the magic circle; then, with a sudden puff, it turned itself into a cloud of smoke.

The smoke rose into the air and the magic circle rose with it, Ben-Muzzy, twins, knapsacks and all. The oak trees were left standing as before.

Chapter Four

"Are we here?" said Joel.

"Is this it?" said Gemma.

They stared around, in wonderment. They were in a land that looked like a picture postcard. The grass was emerald green, the sky bright blue, with a few puffy, pure white clouds and a shining yellow sun.

"Well?" said Joel. "Is it?"

Ben-Muzzy did his best to look careless and unconcerned. "Is it what?"

"Your place," said Gemma.

"Where you were supposed to be taking us," said Joel.

There was a pause.

"Oh, dear," said Gemma. "I think something must have gone wrong."

"*Again*?" said Joel. "So where are we, then?"

Ben-Muzzy swallowed. "I'm afraid I d-don't know."

"You don't know? You bring us somewhere and then you say you don't know? Well, really!" said Joel. "This is too much!"

Ben-Muzzy hung his head.

"Don't cry!" said Gemma. "We can always try again."

"Try again?" said Joel. "Are you crazy?"

"Well, what do you suggest?"

"I think we should go home," said Joel. "We'll make another magic circle, and we'll just go straight back home. I've had enough of this."

"But we've hardly even started! I don't think that's fair. We promised Ben-Muzzy we'd help him. We should at least let him try out a different spell." Gemma turned to Ben-Muzzy. "You do know different spells," she said, "don't you?"

"Oh, I know them," said Ben-Muzzy.

"So what's the problem?" said Joel.

"Well—" said Ben-Muzzy, in a great big apologetic rush, "when you form magic circles and do special sorts of spells like going to different places, it's all very complicated and uses up a great deal of magic. It's not like producing white rabbits out of top hats. Why, you could produce white rabbits out of top hats every single minute of the day, if you felt like it. But spells-for-coming-and-going drain away all your magic . . . they're very powerful spells," said Ben-Muzzy desperately. "I haven't even learned them correctly yet."

"In that case," said Gemma kindly, "I think it's extremely amazing and wonderful that you can do them at all."

"Well, I don't," said Joel. "Not if it means we've got to be stuck here for the rest of our lives."

"I hadn't thought of that!" said Gemma, alarmed.

"No, and you don't have to," said Ben-Muzzy, cheering up slightly. "No one said anything about being stuck here. It's only a question of waiting till the magic comes back into me again."

"Thank goodness for that!" said Gemma. "How long is it likely to take?"

"Not long," said Ben-Muzzy. "There's a little creeping back already."

"Will it go on creeping if you walk around, or do you have to lie down or something?"

"No, I can walk around all right," said Ben-Muzzy.

"Great!" Gemma twirled excitedly. "Let's go and explore! Do you realize,"—she punched her twin on the shoulder—"we could be in another world!"

They started off along a road that looked like green velvet, Gemma leading the way. An old lady was coming toward them. She looked like an ordinary old lady, so that for a moment Gemma was disappointed. Suppose they weren't in another world at all, but simply in a different part of the United States like Peoria, Illinois, or Oshkosh, Wisconsin?

She jabbed Joel in the ribs and prodded him forward. "Go on," she said. "Ask her."

"Excuse me," said Joel politely. "I wonder if you could very kindly tell us where we are?"

The old lady smiled at him. "Just keep on walking," she said, "and in a few minutes you'll come to Wishful Thinking."

"Wishful Thinking?" said Gemma.

"That's right." The old lady studied them a moment. "Are you strangers here? In that case you'd better go straight to the reception office

and ask for your wishes."

"Wishes?" said the twins together.

"What sort of wishes?" Ben-Muzzy wanted to know.

"Just ordinary wishes," said the old lady. "Visitors' wishes. You're entitled to three." She sighed, set her shopping basket on the ground, and took a bright red ping-pong ball out of her pocket. "I wish the bus would hurry up and come," she said.

The red ping-pong ball exploded with a tiny popping sound. Almost immediately, a small yellow bus appeared around the bend in the road. The old lady picked up her shopping basket and nodded cheerfully. "Goodbye," she said. "I hope you enjoy your visit."

Ben-Muzzy and the twins walked on in thoughtful silence.

Gemma was thinking, well, it's not Peoria . . .

"Wow!" said Joel, at last. "Three wishes! I wonder if they'll work?"

"Hers did," said Gemma.

A grin spread itself over Joel's face. "Let's go and get 'em quick, before we have to move on!"

The twins started off at a jog. Ben-Muzzy followed a little more slowly. He wasn't sure that he approved of wishes. It seemed almost like cheating, to a wizard.

At the end of the green velvet road was a large sign, which said:

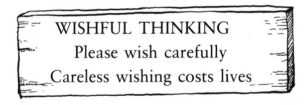

WISHFUL THINKING
Please wish carefully
Careless wishing costs lives

A little further on was another sign, which said:

RECEPTION OFFICE this way
Visitors register here ➡

Joel and Gemma were already busy registering when Ben-Muzzy arrived. An important-looking man sitting at a large desk was taking their details.

"I don't know how long you're staying," he said, "but you'll get your three wishes and not another wish more. If you choose to use them all up in the first five minutes, that's your problem. It won't be any good coming and complaining to me when someone wishes you had purple hair or blue arms. Visitors must take their chances, the same as everyone else."

Blue arms? thought Gemma. Why on earth would anyone wish a stupid thing like that?

"They do," said the man, reading her thoughts. "You'd be surprised." He turned to Ben-Muzzy. "I suppose you want some as well?" he said.

Ben-Muzzy gave his cloak a little hitch. "I don't know that I do," he said. "I'm a wizard. What would I do with wishes?"

"Just as you like, but don't come whining to me when someone turns you into a walking stick."

"You might as well take them," said Joel. "Gemma and I can use them if you don't want them."

"Incidentally," said the man, "a word of warning: The penalty for stealing wishes is very severe. Anyone caught stealing a wish is taken to the High Court, where he is wished into being something useful, such as a children's wading pool or a hospital bed, whatever we happen to be short of at the time. He stays like that for the rest of the year. Some people are never the same again." He handed Ben-Muzzy his card. "I just thought I'd tell you," he said.

They left the reception office and followed another sign that read "Collect your Wishes Here," with an arrow pointing down the road.

"There'll be trouble if anyone tries wishing me into a wading pool!" said Ben-Muzzy, setting his tall black wizard's hat at a jaunty angle.

"Why?" said Joel. "What would you do? Suppose you got turned into a wading pool before you could say a spell. Can wizards say spells when they've been turned into wading pools?"

"I don't know." Ben-Muzzy looked at Joel, aghast. "I never thought of that. Oh, this is horrible! I wish we'd never come here. Let's creep very quietly away where there aren't any people and just wait for my magic to come back."

"But don't you see?" said Gemma triumphantly. "There isn't any need for your magic to come back. We can collect our wishes and use them, all except one, and then when we've only got one left we can wish ourselves wherever we want to!"

"So we can!" Ben-Muzzy beamed. "What a very good idea! How clever of me to bring us here!"

But when they collected their wishes, they found that it was not as simple as Gemma had thought. They were each given three pink ping-pong balls and a card of instructions. On the card of instructions it said:

VISITORS' WISHES
RULES AND REGULATIONS

1. No visitor shall receive more than three wishes in the course of one year.

2. No visitor is allowed to take his wishes out of the country nor use his wishes to take himself out of the country.

3. With reference to Rule and Regulation (2) above, any visitor attempting to make use of his wishes in said manner will be automatically transmuted.

By Order, Wish Master General

"What's automatically transmuted?" Gemma wanted to know.

"Automatically turned into something else?" said Joel.

"Yes, like a wading pool." Ben-Muzzy had become glum again. "Oh, this is horrible!"

"Doesn't matter. By the time we've had nine wishes and used them all up, your magic will probably have come back." Gemma clutched one of her pink ping-pong balls and screwed up her face with excitement. "I'm going to wish for an Old English sheepdog!"

"No!" screamed Ben-Muzzy.

Gemma stared at him. "Why not?"

"Because you won't be able to take it back with you! Magic circles are for three people, not four. If you wish for one of these sheep things, it'll make four!"

"Oh . . . all right, then! I know!" Gemma held out her ping-pong ball and closed her eyes tightly. "I wish I had a rainbow hair flare in pink, lemon, and purple!"

The ping-pong ball burst into nothingness. Gemma opened her eyes. "Where is it?" she wailed. She put up a hand. "Oh!" Draped over

Gemma's head was a long silky wig in violent stripes of different colors. On the top of it was a frilly pink pom-pom. "Oh, awesome!" cried Gemma. She'd wanted a striped wig for ages, but her mother had always shuddered and said no. "I wish I had a mirror!"

"You idiot!" screamed Joel, but it was too late: With a loud *pop!* another of Gemma's ping-pong balls had exploded.

"Well, at least I can see myself," said Gemma, looking at her striped wig in a small hand mirror which had just conveniently appeared.

Ben-Muzzy stood watching gloomily. "This is horrible," he said.

"I think it's fun," said Gemma.

They walked on down the main street. A man was standing at the corner holding half a dozen ping-pong balls.

"He's going to make a wish," said Gemma. "Let's stay and see what he wishes for."

The man held up one of the ping-pong balls. "I wish," he said in bored tones, "that the sky would fall down."

Immediately there was a rushing sound and a large chunk of blue hit the ground with a thump. Looking up, Gemma could see very clearly that there was a small hole in the sky, with blackness showing through it.

The man held up another ping-pong ball. "Now I wish it would go back again," he said simply.

The chunk of blue rose up into the air. Gemma watched it flying higher and higher, until at last it fitted itself neatly into the hole.

"Well, really!" she said. "What a stupid wish!"

The man looked across at her. "Do you mind?" he said. "What business is it of yours, anyway? I've a good mind to wish you into an earthworm. In fact, I shall if there's any more rudeness."

Gemma gulped. "I b-beg your pardon," she said, "I didn't mean to be rude. It's just that I've never seen anyone make a piece of the sky fall down before."

"I do it all the time," said the man, yawning. "One likes to have a hobby of some sort."

"Yes, of course," agreed Gemma. "It's an extremely interesting hobby. Far more interesting than stamp collecting. I'm surprised more people don't do it."

"More people?" said the man, "I wouldn't want more people to do it."

"No, well," said Gemma, "I mean—"

Joel and Ben-Muzzy pulled her hastily away.

"You really mustn't make personal remarks to people," said Ben-Muzzy urgently. "There's no telling what they might do to you."

They continued on their way down the street. Gemma noticed that there were no stores to be seen anywhere. She remarked on this to Joel.

"Well, of course there aren't!" he said. "What would you need stores for, when all you have to do is wish for things? Just think of it! Instead of not being able to buy an ice-cream cone 'cause you've run out of pocket money, all you'd have to do is say 'I wish I had a thousand ice-cream cones' and there you are, you'd have enough to last you for—"

He broke off, wide-eyed with astonishment. One of the ping-pong balls, which he had stuffed into his pocket, had exploded with a familiar *ping*! and in front of him, bursting up out of the ground, were hundreds upon hundreds of ice-cream cones, each covered with a tiny lid. There seemed to be no end to them. One after another they popped up, until the whole street was full of ice-cream cones.

Gemma giggled. "There you are!" she said. "Now you've got a thousand ice-cream cones, and you'll never be able to eat them all!"

"That's just stupid!" said Joel. He was angry with himself for wasting a wish. Ice-cream cones were all very well, especially if they were strawberry, but what could you do with a thousand of them? "There ought to be a law saying wishes will only come true if you really mean them."

"A little late for that now," said Gemma. "You'd better start eating."

Joel bent down and began removing the lids. There were strawberry ice-cream cones, and chocolate ice-cream cones, and coffee ice-cream cones, and vanilla ice-cream cones, and hazelnut ice-cream cones, and raspberry ice-cream cones, and just about every single sort of ice cream that anyone could ever wish for. Joel set rapidly to work on them.

Gemma and Ben-Muzzy watched him greedily.

"Wizards like ice-cream cones," said Ben-Muzzy after a while.

"Do they like vanilla ice-cream cones?" asked Joel.

"Yes," said Ben-Muzzy. "They like any kind of ice cream."

"All right," said Joel generously. "You can have some if you want."

Gemma and Ben-Muzzy began collecting ice-cream cones as fast as they could. For a long time they ate in silence, and Gemma stopped and straightened up.

"It's funny," she said, "but I don't think I like ice cream as much as I used to."

"I was just thinking the same thing myself," agreed Ben-Muzzy. "I'm not sure that ice cream is good for wizards."

"So if," said Gemma to Joel, "you could just very quickly eat a few hundred more—"

Joel groaned. "I've had enough lousy ice cream to last me a lifetime," he said. "I don't think it's very good ice cream. It makes you feel sort of sick."

"I told you you wouldn't be able to get through them all," said Gemma.

She swished her rainbow flare and began crunching her way across the remaining hundreds of ice-cream cones, with Joel and Ben-Muzzy following slowly behind.

As they reached dry land again, a boy came up to them.

"Hey, you!" he said. "Are those your ice-cream cones?"

"They were," said Joel. "But I'm done with them. You can have them, if you like."

"I don't want them," said the boy. "But you'd better clean up that mess or you'll be in trouble."

"How can I clean it up? I don't have anything to clean it up with," said Joel.

The boy stared at him in a very peculiar way. "You have wishes, the same as everyone else, don't you? Then you can just wish it was cleaned up!"

"Oh, wish it yourself!" said Joel rudely. He was all filled up with ice cream, and he didn't think he liked this bossy boy. "Wish it yourself!" he said. "Fathead!"

The boy turned purple with rage. "Snot ball!" he retorted. A nasty gleam appeared in his eye. "I wish your nose would turn purple. And I wish you were all covered in spots! So there!"

There were two small explosions. Gemma looked at her twin and gasped: His nose had turned bright purple, and his face was splattered in large pink blotches.

Beside himself with fury, Joel snatched his two remaining wishes from his pocket. "I wish you were bright scarlet all over!" he shouted. "And I wish your ears stuck out!" he added triumphantly.

Gemma and Ben-Muzzy watched in horrified fascination as the bossy boy gradually turned as red as a lobster and his ears began flapping noisily on either side of his head.

"Joel, how could you?" said Gemma.

"Well, he did it to me first," mumbled Joel, ashamed of himself.

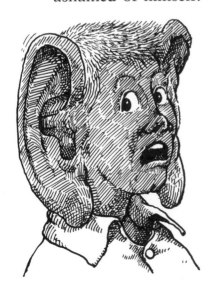 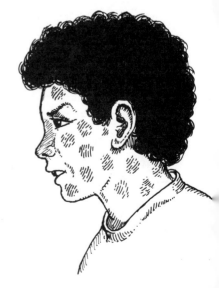

The bossy boy was bossy no longer. Large tears began to roll down his cheeks. "I don't have any m-more wishes left, and now I'll have to s-stay like this until tomorrow!"

He ran off, sobbing, down the street. Gemma looked severely at Joel. "Yes, and you deserve to stay like that, too! All purple and spotted."

"Am I really all purple and spotted?" asked Joel anxiously. He grabbed Gemma's mirror and gave a loud howl.

"It's your own fault," said Gemma. "I don't see why I should waste my last wish getting you back to normal again."

Joel bit his lip very hard. Ben-Muzzy took pity on him.

"Here," he said. "Wizards don't need wishes. You can have mine as long as you promise to use the last one for wishing us away from this town and out into the country, where there aren't any people . . . but make it near trees."

Joel eagerly snatched Ben-Muzzy's three ping-pong balls. "I wish my nose would go back to being its normal color, and I wish all the spots would go away," he gabbled. He turned to Gemma. "Am I all right again?"

"I suppose so," said Gemma, watching critically as the purple faded and the spots disappeared.

"Now get us away from here," urged Ben-Muzzy. "Quickly! Before you have a quarrel with someone else."

Joel clutched the last ping-pong ball firmly in his hand. "I wish we were out in the country near some trees," he said.

For a moment nothing happened; then slowly everything around them was blotted out by a thick mist, and Gemma clutched her twin's hand and held onto it very tightly.

When the mist cleared they found themselves standing on a hilltop, surrounded by emerald green fields. Ben-Muzzy gave a sigh of relief.

"Look," he said, pointing. "There are woods over there. Let's walk across to them and see if we can find some oak trees."

They started off down the hill and across the fields. The woods were farther away than they had thought, and by the time they reached them Gemma was feeling hot and tired and a little bit sick. All the ice cream she had eaten seemed to be churning around inside her in a most disagreeable way.

They entered the woods and began searching for oak trees.

"My magic has definitely come back," said Ben-Muzzy happily. "I feel simply full of magic. I feel as if I could do absolutely any sort of spell that anyone cared to ask me."

Gemma groaned. "I wish I didn't feel so sick," she said. "Maybe you could think of a spell for making people that have eaten too much ice cream not to have eaten too much ice cream, if you know what I mean? Maybe—"

She broke off with a squeak and clapped a hand to her pocket, just as the last of her ping-pong balls exploded with a tiny *pop!*

"Oh!" wailed Gemma at the top of her voice. "Oh, I've gone and wasted my last wish! And I was going to wish for a Sindy Boutique like Tracey Onslow has!"

Joel smiled smugly: He couldn't help feeling just a little pleased that his twin had been as foolish as he had.

"You shouldn't have eaten so much ice cream," he told her. "If you hadn't eaten so much ice cream you wouldn't have felt sick, and then you wouldn't have had to wish that you didn't feel sick, and then you wouldn't have wasted your last wish and—oops!" exclaimed Joel in amazement.

Not looking where he was going, he had bumped headlong into a small fat man wearing yellow check pants, who was coming up the narrow woodland path toward him. Joel sat down with a bump on one side of the path, the

fat man sat down with a bump on the other. Unfortunately he sat in a large pool of muddy water.

"Look what you've done to my pants!" he cried shrilly. "Oh, just look what you've done to my pants! They were new pants, I only wished for them yesterday. Now I shall have to waste another wish getting another pair. Bless my soul, how can you be so careless?"

"I'm sorry," said Joel, though it had been as much the man's fault as his.

"Sorry! Sorry! What's the use of being sorry? That won't make my pants clean again, will it?"

"I'm ever so sorry," said Joel again.

Gemma and Ben-Muzzy were hiding among the trees, frantically beckoning Joel to follow them, but the fat man caught him by the arm and held him back.

"Don't just stand there saying you're sorry. Do something about it! Wish me a new pair!"

"I—can't," stammered Joel. "I don't have any more wishes left, and I'm only a visitor, and—and—"

"I see." The fat man breathed heavily. "I see! You come here, to a land where you don't belong, you ruin other people's new pants by pushing them into puddles of mud, and then you refuse to do anything about it!"

His voice was shriller than ever: It was plain that he was extremely angry. "Well, I don't like that kind of behavior, and what's more I won't put up with it! Little boys like you need punishing. I wish you were a puddle of mud yourself, sir, and a very good day to you, sir!"

The fat man whisked himself away through the woods, as Gemma gave a terrified scream and clutched Ben-Muzzy: Instead of one puddle there were two—and one of them was Joel.

"Oh!" Gemma burst into tears of horror. "What are we going to do? We don't have any wishes left!"

Chapter Five

"Don't cry," said Ben-Muzzy. "Please don't cry. There must be something we can do, if only I can think of it."

Ben-Muzzy was feeling guilty. He was the one who had brought the twins here.

"You're supposed to be a wizard," sobbed Gemma. "Can't you say a spell and bring him back?"

Ben-Muzzy remembered the time he had turned Podnock into a black beetle by mistake. He remembered that Wollibar had had to call in two other Grand Highs before he could turn him back into being Podnock again.

"It's extremely advanced sort of magic," he said. "I haven't really gotten to that stage yet."

"But surely you could try?" pleaded Gemma. "It wouldn't hurt just to try?"

Ben-Muzzy pursed his lips. "You never know what's going to happen when you start playing around with spells like that . . . I might turn him into almost anything."

"Well, whatever you turn him into," said Gemma, starting to cry again, "it couldn't be worse than a puddle of mud!"

Gemma walked over to the puddle and sank down by its side. Her tears splashed mournfully into it. How could she go home without Joel? He was her twin, and everyone knew that twins meant something special to each other, even if they did spend most of their time quarreling.

Ben-Muzzy cleared his throat. "You really need a magic circle," he said, "and some black cats. But if you're willing to take a chance"— Gemma sniffed miserably—"I'll see what I can do. But just remember . . . I can't promise anything!"

Ben-Muzzy removed his hat and set it on the ground. Then he closed his eyes and began walking around it in a circle, chanting to himself:

> "Iggly oogly wubbly ub,
> Into a boy this puddle of mud.
> Iggly oogly wubbly in,
> Change it back to Gemma's twin."

Gemma watched breathlessly as a curious blue light settled itself over the mud. The next moment there was a flash, and where the mud had been now stood a small red squirrel with a bushy tail and bright eyes.

Gemma's face fell. It was a beautiful squirrel, but it wasn't Joel.

"Well, it's better than it was," said Ben-Muzzy hopefully. "I'll try again and see what happens."

He started off once more in a circle. For a few moments he was silent and frowning, and then he began chanting again:

"Iggly oogly wubbly wirrel,
Into a boy turn this squirrel.
Iggly oogly wubbly in,
Change it back to Gemma's twin."

The squirrel disappeared in another flash of blue light. In its place appeared a fluffy yellow chick. Tears began rolling down Gemma's face again. Ben-Muzzy wiped a hand across his forehead.

"I'll try once more," he said bravely. "This is using up an awful lot of magic."

"Perhaps you're doing it wrong?" suggested Gemma between sobs.

"I'm not doing it wrong," said Ben-Muzzy. "It's the right spell, it's just that it's not powerful enough. I told you, it needs a magic circle to make it right."

He began chanting again:

"Iggly oogly wubbly ick,
Into a boy change this chick.
Iggly oogly wubbly in,
Change it back to Gemma's twin."

Gemma gave a scream: The fluffy yellow chick had changed into a brown striped caterpillar!

"Oh, stop it, stop it!" she begged. "You're making him smaller and smaller!"

"I'm sorry," said Ben-Muzzy. "It must be all the magic I'm using up. The spell gets weaker each time I say it."

"Then you'd better not say it any more." Gemma picked up the striped caterpillar and set it on the back of her hand. "We must do something quickly! He'll be changing into a butterfly before we know where we are."

Ben-Muzzy settled his hat back on his head. He had the impression that his head was definitely shrinking. "There's only one thing we can do . . . we'll have to walk around until we find someone who's willing to make a magic circle with us. A dog or a cat would do, if we can't find a person. Animals are quite good at magic circles."

"And then what?" said Gemma.

"Then we can all go home," said Ben-Muzzy, simply, "and Wollibar will be able to change him back again."

Gemma thought about it. She shook her head. "I don't think that's a good idea. Suppose you can't remember the right spell again? We'd end up goodness knows where, and Joel would still be a caterpillar and you'd just go on making him smaller and smaller until he disappeared altogether."

"So what do you suggest we do?" asked Ben-Muzzy sulkily.

"I'll tell you what we're going to do." Gemma stood up, still holding the caterpillar. "We're going to go and steal a couple of wishes."

"B-b-b-b-but they'll t-t-t-turn us into wading pools!" gasped Ben-Muzzy.

"No, they won't," said Gemma. "That's why we're stealing two. With the first one we're going to wish ourselves right at the edge of this horrible place—because it must have an edge, somewhere. Then as soon as we're safely out we can wish Joel back to being himself again."

"But that's against the rules!" said Ben-Muzzy.

Gemma tossed her head. "You think I care about them and their stupid rules?"

"You will when you've been automatically transmuted!" Gemma frowned. She had forgotten, for a moment, what automatically transmuted meant.

"You know what'll happen?" said Ben-Muzzy. "The minute you steal a wish and wish us somewhere else, the person you stole it from will simply wish us right back again and then we'll both be turned into wading pools!"

Gemma had not thought of this. "Oh!" she said. "You've just got a thing about wading pools!"

"Well, I don't want to be turned into one," said Ben-Muzzy.

"Neither do I," said Gemma. "So we'll just have to be extra careful and make sure we do it without anyone noticing . . . of course, if you were a *real* wizard you could make yourself invisible."

"I *am* a real wizard and I *can* make myself invisible!" Ben-Muzzy drew himself up very straight and stiff. "I did it for my exam—at least," he remembered, "I nearly did it. I would have done it, if I hadn't said the spell backward. But I know how to say it forward all right."

"Well, there you are!" said Gemma. "It's easy as pie! You can make yourself invisible and steal a couple of wishes without anyone noticing a thing! Let's go and do it immediately."

She started off through the woods with Joel in one of the pockets of the knapsack and Ben-Muzzy trotting unhappily at her side.

"The thing is," he said, "I only have just about

enough magic left . . . I mean, I won't have enough magic left to bring myself back again."

"Well, that's all right," said Gemma. "You can stay invisible until you get some more."

"But it isn't good for you to remain invisible too long," said Ben-Muzzy. "A friend of Podnock's once knew a wizard that turned himself invisible and stayed like that so long he couldn't ever get back. He had to be invisible for the rest of his life. There are very strict rules about making yourself invisible," said Ben-Muzzy desperately. "You're not supposed to do it more than once a day and you're not supposed to stay like that for more than half an hour."

"Well, surely, by the end of half an hour you'll have enough magic to make yourself visible again?"

"I might have," said Ben-Muzzy. "But then again, I might not. And anyway, I'm not sure I like this idea. It's dangerous, and it's not good to steal things."

"Who cares?" cried Gemma. "I'm not going to let Joel stay a caterpillar and turn into a butterfly and die! And I really don't see," she added, "what harm it can do to steal two measly wishes from people that have so many they go around turning people into puddles of mud!"

Ben-Muzzy really couldn't think of any answer to that.

They left the woods and walked along a narrow lane. At the end of the lane was a collection of small cottages. Two woman were standing outside one of them, talking. As Gemma passed, she could see that both women had pockets bulging with red ping-pong balls. She nudged Ben-Muzzy.

"There you are . . . they've got so many wishes, I bet they don't know what to do with them. You can take one from each of them and I don't suppose they'll even notice they're gone."

Ben-Muzzy nodded gloomily. They walked away from the houses and stopped around the corner of the lane.

"I'll wait here for you," said Gemma. "As soon as you've got them, you can run back and get me and we'll wish ourselves right to the edge of the land."

Ben-Muzzy clamped his hat firmly on his head and concentrated all his remaining magic on the spell for making himself invisible. This time, he

must remember to say it forward and not backward!

Gemma watched in fascination as Ben-Muzzy slowly began to disappear. First his feet and then his hands and then the rest of him, until only the tip of his hat could be seen.

"Am I all gone?" asked Ben-Muzzy, anxiously.

"All except a piece of your hat," Gemma told him.

"That's because I've run out of magic again. You'd better hold it for me."

The tip of Ben-Muzzy's hat rose into the air and came toward Gemma, who giggled nervously as she took it. It was a strange feeling, to hold an invisible hat.

"All right," said Ben-Muzzy. "I'm going now. Wait here for me."

Ben-Muzzy crept silently back down the lane until he came to the houses. The two women were still talking. Holding his breath, he dipped a hand into each of their pockets and lifted out two ping-pong balls. The women noticed nothing. Still holding his breath, Ben-Muzzy tiptoed back again.

All went well until a small girl came out of a cottage. She stared at the two ping-pong balls, apparently floating through the air by themselves, and then she made a sudden snatch at them. Ben-Muzzy took to his heels and ran. The small girl, squeaking with excitement, ran after him.

"Quick!" panted Ben-Muzzy, seizing Gemma's hand. "Someone's after me!"

The small girl turned the corner. She stopped as she saw Gemma. The ping-pong balls were floating in the air by her side.

"Here!" said the small girl accusingly. "Those aren't your wishes! Only grown-ups have red wishes. You're not a grown up!"

"I wish that Gemma and Joel and I were right at the edge of this land!" gabbled Ben-Muzzy breathlessly.

The small girl opened her eyes very wide as a mist gradually rose up around Gemma and the one remaining ping-pong ball. They heard her running back down the lane, shouting at the top of her voice: "Ma! Ma! Someone's stealing wishes!"

Inside the swirling mist, Gemma shivered. Ben-Muzzy clutched her hand tighter.

"As soon as we get there, we'll run into the next land before they can call us back again," he said reassuringly.

"Yes," said Gemma; but inside herself she was thinking, suppose they won't let us through? Suppose they call us back before we get there.

Ben-Muzzy was thinking the same thing.

The mist began to clear again, and they stood waiting, wondering where they would be. Would they still be in the same place, in the lane, near the row of cottages, with the small girl standing accusingly in front of them? What would happen to them? Would they be taken to the High Court and turned into wading pools?

"Look! Look!"

Gemma was almost sobbing with relief. Ben-Muzzy peered through the fading mist and saw a large signpost which said:

EDGE OF WISHING LAND
DANGER PAST THIS POINT

"I don't care if there is danger!" declared Gemma. "I'm not staying here another minute!"

Chapter Six

Gemma and Ben-Muzzy were floating. They had stepped over the edge of Wishing Land into complete nothingness. Curiously enough, it wasn't the least bit frightening. Currents of air supported them, bouncing them upward, toppling them downward; and if they fell off it scarcely mattered, for all about them were clouds, big and billowy, soft as dishcloths. Sinking into a cloud was like sinking into an armchair made of cotton.

"This is very strange," said Gemma, sliding down an air current. "I suppose in a minute we'll wake up."

"Wake up?" said Ben-Muzzy. "I'm not asleep!"

"Are you sure?" said Gemma. "I thought it might be a dream."

"Well, it's not," said Ben-Muzzy. He only wished that it were. He was still concerned about having to remain invisible. The wizard that Podnock's friend had known had had to paint his face and hands with pink paint in the end so that people could see him.

"In that case," said Gemma. "I think we should use that other wish, quickly, before Joel starts turning into a chrysalis." She took the caterpillar out of her knapsack. "Do you have it?"

Ben-Muzzy opened his hand. "Oh," he said. And then, "*Oh*."

"What is it?" cried Gemma. "Don't say you've gone and lost it?"

"Certainly not," said Ben-Muzzy.

"So why did you say *oh* like that?"

"Because I think I've discovered what the catch is . . . I think these wishes must be made to self-destruct."

"You mean you've squashed it!"

"I mean it's all shriveled up to nothing . . . it's just a nasty sticky mess. Like glue. Like—"

Before Ben-Muzzy could finish there was a muffled shout from somewhere near Gemma's right ear: "What's going on?"

"Joel!" shrieked Gemma. She made a grab for

him with the hand which had been holding the caterpillar. Joel hung in space, rubbing his eyes and looking bewildered.

"Where are we?" he said. "Have I been asleep? I've been having the most peculiar dreams . . . I dreamt I was all kinds of different things."

"You were!" said Gemma. "Just a second ago you were a caterpillar!"

"I thought I was," said Joel. "So what are we doing now?"

"Now we're floating through space," said Gemma.

"Oh, I see," said Joel; and then: "No, I don't! What are we doing that for?"

"Because we've escaped—Ben-Muzzy very kindly turned himself invisible. The only trouble is, he's run out of magic and he thinks he might have to stay invisible forever."

"Doesn't look very invisible to me," said Joel.

Gemma turned her head. "You're right! He's come back!"

"I have?" Ben-Muzzy patted himself anxiously. "Are you sure?"

"Positive!" said Gemma. She dug a hand into the knapsack, intending to take out her mirror so that he could check. The mirror was not there: neither was the rainbow hair flare.

"Oh!" wailed Gemma. "My things are all gone!"

"Obviously,"—Ben-Muzzy happily waved his hands to and fro in front of his face—"*every*thing is made to self-destruct . . . bad things as well as good."

"So you couldn't go there and wish for a million dollars and take it home with you even if you wanted," said Joel. "That's a pity."

After a while, the dishcloth clouds began to disappear and they found themselves sinking slowly earthwards, through a layer of blue.

"This," said Joel, hitting the ground with a slight thump, "must be how it feels to parachute."

Gemma and Ben-Muzzy landed one on either side of him. Gemma was the first to scramble to her feet. She was about to take a step forward when she gave a little horrified squeak, jumped backward instead, crashed into Ben-Muzzy and went bouncing off onto Joel.

"What d'you do that for?" said Joel angrily.

Gemma pointed. "L-look!"

"Oh, wow!" said Joel.

They seemed to have landed on the side of a mountain. They could see the ground spread out far below them.

"Now what do we do?" Gemma sank down, huddling as far from the edge as possible. The others followed suit.

"This is very peculiar," said Joel with a frown. "If this is a mountain, what are these tall green things growing all around us?"

"They look like blades of grass," said Gemma. "Except," she added, "that they're too tall." They were taller even than the mountain. "Maybe they're a sort of tree."

"Green trees?"

"I suppose there isn't any reason why you

shouldn't have a green tree . . . maybe they're not ripe yet."

Ben-Muzzy cleared his throat. "A-hem," he said.

The twins looked up.

"I think," said Ben-Muzzy, "that *those* are trees."

There was an awed silence. In the distance stood a cluster of oaks. They were like no other oaks that the twins had ever seen. They were giant oaks, taller than the tallest skyscraper; so tall that the topmost branches were almost lost among the clouds.

"Cripes!" said Joel.

"And look!" squealed Gemma. "Look at that!"

Joel looked, and his jaw dropped open. Gemma was pointing to something that was, quite unmistakably, a buttercup, nodding its head above the enormous blades of grass.

"Just look at the size of its petals! They're like soup plates!"

"I don't understand this," said Joel, getting worried. "Even in the jungle you don't get plants as big as that."

"And anyway," said Gemma, "buttercups don't grow in jungles."

"Perhaps it isn't a buttercup. Perhaps it's—"

Joel broke off in alarm as Gemma suddenly screamed and clutched him. All three threw themselves flat on the ground as a huge flying object passed overhead, its wings making a vigorous whirring sound, its body casting an enormous shadow, cutting out the light of the sun. It zoomed over them and landed in the center of the buttercup.

"What is it, what is it?" whispered Gemma.

Cautiously, Joel lifted his head. "It's a—it's a—a bee!" he discovered.

"But it can't be!" wailed Gemma. "It's as big as we are!"

"Or we're as small as it," said Ben-Muzzy.

The twins said nothing for a moment. Ben-Muzzy had turned very pale. It made them feel uncomfortable.

"I'm just the same size I always was," said Joel.

"It's not us that's changed," said Gemma. "It's everything else that's bigger."

Ben-Muzzy scrambled carefully to his feet and

gazed out across the surrounding countryside.

"I have a horrible idea," he said, "that I know where we are."

"W-where?" said Gemma.

Ben-Muzzy removed his hat and wiped his forehead with the edge of his cloak. "If I'm right," he said, "we're in the Land of the Ogre and the Giant."

"Yikes!" said Joel. "We'd better get out again, quick!"

He jumped to his feet. Ben-Muzzy and Gemma both lunged at him.

"Don't panic!" Ben-Muzzy grabbed him just in time: Another second and he would have been over the edge. "It might not be as bad as we think. As long as we're in giant territory and not ogre territory, we'll be all right. Giants are quite friendly, you just have to watch they don't tread on you by mistake."

"Are you sure about that?" said Joel.

"Absolutely positive. I remember Wollibar telling me. He spent his summer holidays here last year. He said that giants don't have much brain but they're quite harmless."

"And ogres?" said Gemma carelessly.

Ben-Muzzy turned pale again. "Ogres are different," he said. "Giants are terrified of ogres."

The twins swallowed. In a small voice, Gemma said, "So how do you tell which is a giant and which is an ogre?"

"Giants look just the same as people," said Ben-Muzzy, "except that they're giants, of course. But ogres have long pointed teeth that grow right down over their mouths like elephant tusks, and horrible horny fingernails, and no hair, and red eyes."

"And—what do they do to you?" said Gemma. "If they happen to catch you?"

Ben-Muzzy had no time to reply to Gemma's question. He opened his mouth, but before any sound could come out, the mountain on which they were standing began to move around in the most alarming fashion. It seemed to tear itself up out of the earth by the roots. The ground beneath their feet trembled violently and heaved itself into the air. There was a loud rumbling sound.

"It's an earthquake!" yelled Joel.

The ground seemed to be slipping sideways.

The twins hung on as long as they could, then found themselves flung off and flying through the air. They landed almost on top of one another. For a few minutes they lay there, dazed and shaken, with the thick blades of grass growing as tall as trees all around them.

"Are you all right?" said Gemma. "Where's Ben-Muzzy?"

The stared around for him. Joel gave a yell of horror: The mountain was still moving, and they could see, now, that it wasn't a mountain at all but an enormous giant, looming over them, big as the Empire State Building.

"We were sitting on it!" whispered Gemma

with wide, terrified eyes.

"Sh!" Joel pulled her down into the grass. Is it an ogre or a giant? he was wondering.

And where is Ben-Muzzy? thought Gemma desperately.

And then they saw him, a tiny figure in black hat and yellow cloak, clinging to the top of the giant's boot.(Or the ogre's boot, thought Joel, with a shiver.) Poor Ben-Muzzy! His plight was desperate. If he jumped to the ground, he would surely break his neck, but if he didn't jump he would be carried away with the giant.

The giant stretched his mighty arms to the sky and yawned. Ben-Muzzy nearly fell off his boot in fright. He lost his grip, clawed the air with both hands, and just managed to haul himself back again. But the giant had obviously felt something. He lifted up his leg and turned his head to look at it.

Gemma gave a squawk of terror and covered her face with her hands. The giant had red eyes and a bald head. His front teeth grew down like an elephant's tusks and his fingernails were long and horny. He was not a giant at all: He was an ogre!

The ogre plucked Ben-Muzzy off his boot and held him up to examine him. Joel could see Ben-Muzzy wriggling helplessly in his grasp. The ogre suddenly opened his mouth and roared. His voice rolled over the hills like thunder.

"HO-O-O!" roared the ogre.

"Help!" squeaked Ben-Muzzy.

The ogre closed his fist—and Ben-Muzzy stopped squeaking.

In a matter of seconds the ogre was out of sight, but for a long time afterward the ground shivered and shook.

Gemma took her hands from her face and stared across at Joel. "What are we going to do?" she said. "What are we going to do?"

Joel shook his head gloomily. "Perhaps we're only having a nightmare?" he suggested. "Perhaps all this isn't really happening?"

"But it *is* really happening," said Gemma, "and we couldn't both be having the same nightmare!"

"I don't see why not. We're twins, aren't we?"

"Well, all right, then, if we're having a nightmare, let's stop it and wake up!"

Joel pinched himself very hard and gave a yell.

"You see?" said Gemma. "Oh, poor Ben-Muzzy! What are we going to do?"

"Don't keep saying what are we going to do!" snapped Joel. "How do I know what we're going to do? There's nothing very much we can do. Without Ben-Muzzy to take us away we'll be stuck here forever and ever."

"I'm not thinking of getting away. I'm thinking of Ben-Muzzy!"

"Ben-Muzzy's a wizard," said Joel firmly. "Wizards can look after themselves."

"Ben-Muzzy can't," Gemma pointed out. "He's only a junior wizard."

"Well, he can say a spell, can't he? He can make himself invisible again, or magic the ogre into a tadpole."

"He can't," said Gemma, starting to cry. "He used up all his magic making himself invisible before. And you know his spells always go wrong!"

"Well, I still don't see what we can do about it," said Joel irritably. He only said it irritably because he was worried. Being worried always made him irritable. "For one thing," he said, "we don't know where he's been taken to, and for another thing, even if we did I don't see how we could get there. That—that *ogre* must have covered at least a mile every time it took a step. It's probably thousands of miles away by now. Even if we had our bikes here, which we don't, it'd take us months and months to cover that distance."

Gemma took a breath. "I don't care," she said. "I don't care how far away Ben-Muzzy's gone, we're not just going to sit here and do nothing about it. We're going to find him again *some*how."

"All right," said Joel gloomily. "You tell me how. You just tell me how! I'd be really interested to know how you think we're going to cover hundreds and thousands of miles when we don't even know where he is and we only have our feet to get there on."

Gemma leaned against a blade of grass. She was silent and thoughtful for a while.

"I know what we'll do," she said.

"What?" Joel looked at her suspiciously.

"We'll go and find a giant," said Gemma, "and we'll ask him to help us." Then quickly, before her twin could start objecting: "You know Ben-Muzzy said that giants were friendly."

"Ben-Muzzy also said that giants were terrified of ogres," Joel reminded her.

"They may be terrified of them," said Gemma, "but that doesn't mean to say they won't help us."

"And it doesn't mean to say that they will help us. And anyway, where do you think we're going to find one?"

"I don't know," said Gemma, scrambling to her feet. "We'll just walk around until we see one. They should be easy enough to spot."

She started off through the grass, her chin held very high, her back straight and determined. Joel sighed. He knew it was no use arguing with his twin when she was in this kind of a mood, and in any case he had no ideas of his own to put forward.

It was a peculiar feeling, walking through grass that was as tall as trees.

"Now we know what it must be like to be a beetle," said Gemma.

"It's easier for beetles," said Joel. "They can crawl to the top of things and have a look around. We're stuck down here."

"What I'm scared of," said Gemma, confidingly, "is meeting a wood louse. I'm sure it would be like some awful prehistoric monster. And, oh, help!" she added in a panic. "There's an ant and it's coming straight toward us!"

They leapt out of the way just in time, as a gigantic red ant hurried busily past them. They had never realized before just how terrifying an ant could be.

"Imagine," gasped Joel, "what a stag beetle would look like!"

They had been walking for only about ten minutes when the ground began to shake beneath them. They stopped and looked at each other apprehensively.

"S-something's c-coming," stammered Gemma.

"It could be a giant," said Joel.

"And it could be an ogre," said Gemma.

Joel felt that the time had come for him to take command again.

"We'll wait and see which it is," he said firmly. "If it's an ogre we'll hide behind that stone over there and keep very quiet until it's

gone. If it's a giant, we'll jump up and down and shout at the tops of our voices and try to make him hear us."

The earth was shaking violently now, and they knew that the giant or the ogre, whichever it was, must be nearly on top of them. A large shadow blotted out the sun. Joel and Gemma stood with their heads flung back, staring up through the blades of grass. A great black object came bearing down on them: It was a foot! They threw themselves hurriedly out of the way, in company with two huge ants and a monstrous

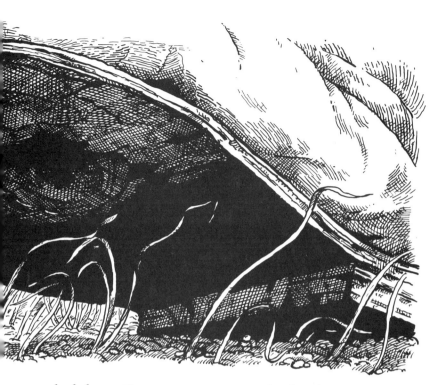

ladybug. Gemma was too excited to be scared of the ants.

"It's a giant, it's a giant!" she cried and began to jump up and down.

"Help, help!" roared the twins together.

The giant stopped in the middle of a stride. He shook his head in bewilderment. There was a curious ringing sound in his ears.

"Help!" yelled the twins, as loudly as they could.

Did I hear someone whisper "help"? thought the giant. He bent over and peered into the grass. The twins saw an enormous eye, like a great blue frying pan, staring at them.

"Help!" said Gemma faintly.

What the giant saw were two tiny creatures, very much alike, dressed in red T-shirts and blue jeans. He had never seen insects like that before. He stretched out a hand and picked them up, very carefully so as not to crush them. Then he held them at eye level and examined them.

Gemma stretched out a trembling hand toward Joel. It was all very well to talk about finding a giant, but now that they had actually found one she wasn't so sure she liked the idea. The giant was breathing gusts of hot air over them, and Gemma kept thinking what a long way it would be to the ground if she fell off.

"What have we here?" boomed the giant.

Joel and Gemma promptly fell over. Joel rolled off the edge of the giant's hand and felt himself falling through space, and then the other hand came out and caught him and he was back with Gemma again.

"Do you mind not talking so loud?" asked Joel, shaking all over like a leaf.

"All right," whispered the giant amiably. "Do

you mind not talking so soft? I can hardly hear you."

"Is that better?" shouted Joel.

"Yes, that's better," said the giant.

He scratched his massive head with its crop of curly hair. He was a pleasant-looking giant. He had big rosy cheeks all covered in freckles, and he was wearing an old woolly sweater with holes.

"That's funny," he said. "I didn't know insects could talk."

"We're not insects!" bellowed Joel. "We're twins!"

"Oh, I see," said the giant, though he obviously didn't. "I'm a giant," he told them.

"I know you are!" shouted Joel. "We've been looking for a giant."

"We're very glad we found you," added Gemma, as loud as she could. "We want you to help us."

"Wait a minute," said the giant. "Can twins fly?"

"No," said Joel.

"I thought they couldn't," said the giant, pleased with himself. "I couldn't see any wings.

I think I'd better lie down, and then if you fall off again you won't have far to go."

Very carefully, the giant lowered himself to the ground. Really, thought Gemma, he was most considerate.

He set them on top of a broad stone and then lay down in the grass with his head a few inches away from them.

"That's better," he said. "Now, what was it you were saying?"

"We want you to help us," said Gemma.

"All right," said the giant. "By the way, my name is Laughable."

"Is it?" said Joel, surprised. "Why? What's so funny about it?"

"It is funny, isn't it?" agreed the giant. He chuckled, and the twins at once fell over again. "I beg your pardon," he said, setting them upright. "It's just that Laughable is a funny name, when you come to think about it. I never considered it before. One of my brothers is Ridiculous. I think that's even funnier, don't you?"

The twins laughed politely. The giant beamed.

"As you were saying?" he asked.

"It's about our friend," roared Joel. His throat was starting to become pretty sore. "He's been captured, you see, and—"

"What are your names?" said Laughable. "Do twins have names?"

"Yes, we're called Joel and Gemma, and as I was saying, it's about our friend—"

"Joelangemma?" repeated Laughable. "Just the one name between you?"

"Yes, that's right," said Joel. It seemed easier than bothering to explain. He did wish Laughable would keep to the point. "Our friend," continued Joel firmly, "has been stolen by an ogre."

"An ogre?" Laughable sat up and stared all around him. "Where is he now?" he whispered hoarsely.

"We don't know, that's the trouble. He set off in that direction, over there, and he took our friend with him."

"I know that ogre," said Laughable, shaking slightly. "His name's Gruck. He's always invading our territory. He's no right to be here at all, but he lives just over the border and he *will* keep breaking the rules. That's what happens with ogres. They know we're scared of them and they deliberately come and terrify us."

"Yes, well, this one's stolen our friend," said Joel "and we want to get him back again."

"You can't," said Laughable sadly.

"Why not?"

"Little creatures like twins wouldn't stand a chance. And how would you get there, anyway? You can't fly, you don't have any wings."

"That's why we wanted a giant," explained Joel. "We wanted a giant to help us."

Laughable shivered. "Giants are scared of ogres. Giants don't go anywhere near them."

"Oh, please help us!" begged Gemma. "It's our only chance! Please, Laughable." She stretched out a hand and stroked one of his fingers. Laughable liked that. He smiled happily. "Will you help us?" coaxed Gemma. "Oh, you will, won't you?"

"I'm scared of ogres," said Laughable.

"Look, all you have to do," said Joel rashly, "is take us to his house and get us inside it; then we'll rescue our friend and you can wait outside and take us back again."

"I'm scared of ogres," repeated Laughable. "They're nasty, cruel creatures. I don't like them. And Gruck is one of the worst."

"You mean you won't help us?" said Gemma, bursting into tears.

Two tears at once trickled down Laughable's face in sympathy. "I'm scared," he muttered.

"So are we," sobbed Gemma, "and we're smaller than you!"

Laughable's tears splashed over the twins in a

tidal wave. Joel moved back a step to avoid being drowned. An idea came to him.

"If you were given one wish," he said to Laughable, "what would you wish for?"

Laughable stopped crying. His big blue frying-pan eyes lit up.

"I would wish for a new woolly jersey," he said, simply. "A green one. I've always wanted a woolly jersey of my own. When you've got six brothers and seven sisters you always have to wear other people's hand-me-downs, and by the time they get to me they're always full of holes. But I don't have a wish"—the tears sprang back into his eyes—"so I'll never have a woolly jersey."

"I'll tell you what," said Joel, ducking for cover beneath a nearby buttercup as Laughable's tears came plopping, "our friend that we want to rescue is a wizard, and if you help us we'll ask him to do a spell to get a woolly jersey for you."

"A green woolly jersey? Without holes?"

"If that's what you want."

"It is," said Laughable. "It's what I want more than anything else in the whole world. Could he really do it, do you think?"

"Oh, yes, it would be perfectly easy for him," said Joel, conveniently forgetting that more often than not Ben-Muzzy's spells went wrong.

Laughable hesitated. "I'm scared of ogres," he said. "But I would like a new woolly jersey."

"A green one," urged Joel.

"Without any holes in it," said Gemma.

"All my own," murmured Laughable. Slowly he sat up. "I'll take you to Gruck's house," he said, "but I don't have to come in with you, do I? Because I'm scared of ogres!"

Chapter Seven

Ben-Muzzy was a prisoner in Gruck's house. He had been placed on a high table covered with a prickly red cloth, and an enormous glass tumbler had been put over him.

Ben-Muzzy had never been so terrified in all his life. He had been bounced up and down in Gruck's pocket, he had been picked up and examined, he had been prodded and poked, and several times he had nearly had all the breath squeezed out of him. His head had been twisted this way and that, his arms and legs had been pulled so hard he had thought they were going to part company with his body, several tufts of hair had been torn from his head. He had only just avoided having his eyes poked out. He was bruised all over and his ribs had been crushed so much that he found it painful to breathe. And all the time, Gruck's red-rimmed eyes had been glimmering evilly at him, and gusts of hot breath blowing over him and scorching him.

It was obvious that the ogre thought he was some new kind of insect, and was puzzled.

"If it were a fly," said Gruck, "I would pull off its wings. If it were an ant, I would stamp on it. And if it were a beetle, I would eat it. But it isn't any of those things."

He set Ben-Muzzy on the table, on the prickly red tablecloth. "It might be good to eat," he said. "But then again, it might not. And I don't want to poison myself."

Ben-Muzzy tried to say that he was a wizard, and that wizards were definitely not good to eat, but he was too terrified to do more than stand and tremble.

"I'll go and ask my friends what it is," decided Gruck. "If it's not poisonous, I'll eat it and see what it tastes like. If it is poisonous, I'll stamp on it."

He picked up a large glass tumbler, turned it upside down, and imprisoned Ben-Muzzy beneath it.

For several minutes after the ogre had left the room, Ben-Muzzy was unable to stop trembling. He could see no way of escape. If he had had any

magic left he could have made himself invisible again, but the little magic that had come back to him had all drained away during the terrifying ride in Gruck's pocket, and by the time it returned it would be too late. The ogre would be back at any moment.

Tears of fright trickled down Ben-Muzzy's face. He would rather have been turned into a black beetle than be captured by an ogre. Even Wollibar had said that ogres were dreadful creatures, and it took a great deal to shake a Grand High.

Ben-Muzzy tried pushing the glass tumbler, but it was too heavy for him. He pushed and pushed with all his might, and still it didn't move.

He kicked at the glass with his foot. He ran from one side of it to the other, he beat against it with his hands, and at last he sank down onto the prickly red tablecloth and burst into great sobs of despair. He was all by himself in the house of this horrible ogre, and no one could rescue him because no one knew where he was. And very soon the horrible ogre would come back, and then Ben-Muzzy would be eaten alive (if he weren't stamped on) and no one would ever know what had happened to him. And for a little while people would go around saying, "Do you remember Ben-Muzzy?" but after a while even Wollibar and Podnock would stop saying it and then he would be quite, quite forgotten . . .

"I'll just put you through the window," said Laughable to the twins. "I can't come in with you because I'm scared of ogres, and I'm more scared of Gruck than any other ogre. But I'll put you through the window and then I'll wait out here for you."

"All right," agreed Joel. "But how will we get out again?"

Laughable scratched his head.

"If you had wings," he said, "you could fly. Little creatures like you should have wings."

"We don't need them," said Gemma. "We're pretty big, in our own land. But I know what we can do . . . if you break off a twig and prop it up against the window, we can use it as a sort of gangplank. And then we can come out again the same way, and you can wait outside for us and hide among the bushes."

Laughable thought this was a very clever idea. He snapped off a twig, which to the twins seemed almost as big as a tree trunk, and he stretched out his arm and propped it up against the window on the ground floor.

"I'd better go and hide now," he said. "If Gruck sees me in his garden he'll chase after me and capture me. And ogres do terrible things to giants."

Poor Laughable was shaking all over.

"OK, you go away and hide," said Joel. "We'll see you in a minute."

Laughable picked them up from the ground and set them on the gangplank, then turned and galloped off through the garden gate, and crouched down behind the wall.

"Don't forget my woolly jersey!" he whispered anxiously.

Joel and Gemma crawled on hands and knees toward the window, trying not to look down at the ground which was getting farther and farther away from them. The window was open just a crack, but the crack was large enough for the twins to climb through it. They stood on the ledge and gazed around. Suddenly Gemma gave a squeak and clutched Joel's arm.

"There's Ben-Muzzy! Look! Over there!"

"Yikes," said Joel. "He has a glass jar over him. I hope he can breathe all right."

Ben-Muzzy was sitting on the prickly red cloth with his head in his hands. He hadn't seen the twins. Joel and Gemma began jumping up and down on the window ledge, waving their arms to attract attention. It seemed a very long time before Ben-Muzzy looked up. When at last he did, an expression of amazement came over his face. He scrambled to his feet and pressed his nose to the glass, staring across at the twins as if he could hardly believe they were real. Then he began gesticulating with his hands, and they could see his lips moving.

"I wonder what he's trying to tell us?" said Gemma.

"Dunno."

Joel was busy searching for some way in which they could reach the table. They could jump from the window ledge into an armchair in the center of the room, and they could jump from the armchair onto a woolly rug on the floor, but then the top of the table would tower above them as high as a mountain and they would have no way of climbing up to it.

"In any case," said Gemma, following his thoughts, as the twins sometimes did with each other, "even if we could manage to get on the table I don't think we'd be able to push the glass over. You have to remember," she said sadly, "that we're no bigger than black beetles, and have you ever seen a black beetle that was strong enough to do a thing like that?"

As if to confirm her words, Ben-Muzzy began battering against the sides of the glass, then stopped and shook his head helplessly. He was quite plainly telling the twins that they could not hope to rescue him that way.

"What we need—," said Joel. He dug a hand deep into one of the pockets of his jeans. "What we need," he said triumphantly, "is marbles!"

Gemma was not so sure. The marbles were very small and the glass tumbler very large. Also it was a very long way off.

"You'd never be able to hit it from here!"

She was probably right: She usually was. Joel needed to get closer.

"You stay here," he said. "I'll see if I can jump into that chair."

The chair was in the middle of the room. Joel wasn't at all certain that he could jump that far. If he missed, he would go crashing to the ground and probably break every bone in his body.

"Be careful," urged Gemma.

Joel took a deep breath and jumped. The chair loomed up at him. It was a big comfortable chair. Joel landed squarely in the middle of it, bounced up and down a few times like a rubber ball, and then rolled into the corner. He picked himself up and waved at Gemma.

"It's fun," he called. "It's like being on a trampoline."

"Well, then, I'm coming too," said Gemma. Truth to tell, she was a little scared, being left

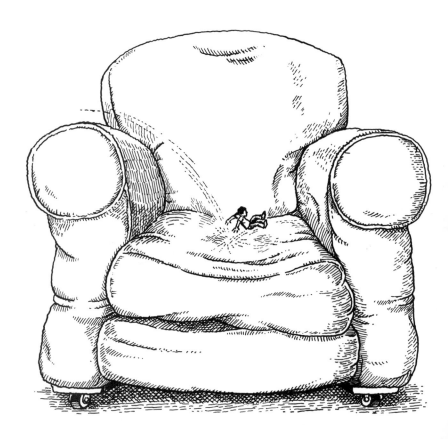

stranded on the window ledge by herself. "Watch out, or I'll land on you."

Gemma came flying through the air. Joel ducked and rolled out of the way as his twin bounced down beside him. Ben-Muzzy watched them anxiously, wondering what they were trying to do. Gruck would be back at any moment, and here were the twins jumping up and down and giggling!

Joel stood up and balanced himself carefully near the edge of the chair. He made throwing motions at Ben-Muzzy and then covered his head with his hands and ducked down. Ben-Muzzy wondered if perhaps Joel was going mad. The next moment a small glass marble came flying across the room and missed the glass by a couple of inches.

"Drat!" said Joel.

He tried again. This time, the marble found its mark: A large crack appeared in the glass. Gemma gave a cry of excitement and clapped a hand to her mouth. Ben-Muzzy understood now what Joel was trying to do. He knelt down on the prickly red cloth, covered his head with his hands, and pulled his cloak around him.

"This is my last marble," said Joel.

He pulled back his arm and took careful aim. The marble flew across the room, hit the top of the glass with a loud crash, and splinters showered in all directions.

Ben-Muzzy was free! He picked his way cautiously through the large pieces of broken glass and walked to the edge of the table. As he did so, there was a heavy tramping of feet along the passage outside.

"It's the ogre!" gasped Ben-Muzzy. "He's come back!"

"Quick! Jump onto the chair with us and hide!"

Ben-Muzzy didn't even stop to think about it:

He threw himself off the table, hurtled through the air, and bounced down beside the twins.

"In here!" said Gemma.

She had discovered that one of the cushions was coming apart at the seams. She crawled through the hole into the darkness and floundered through a sea of feathers, trying not to sneeze. Joel and Ben-Muzzy crawled in after her. The edge of Ben-Muzzy's cloak had just been whisked through the hole when the door opened.

"What's all this?" said Gruck's voice, very loudly.

"It's broken the glass and escaped," said another voice.

"It couldn't possibly have broken the glass all by itself," objected Gruck. "It was only a little thing, the size of a black beetle. A little yellow thing with a pointed head. It must still be in the room somewhere. Don't worry, I'll find it. And when I find it, I'll pull it to pieces, bit by bit!"

Heavy footsteps banged around the floor. Furniture was dragged this way and that. The cushion in which the twins and Ben-Muzzy were hiding was picked up and shaken very violently.

Gemma was tossed up and down in the darkness. Feathers tickled her face and flew up her nose, and either Joel or Ben-Muzzy was thrown on top of her. She felt sure she was going to suffocate. The cushion was flung back onto the chair, and for a terrifying moment Gemma had a vision of an ogre sitting on top of it and crushing the life out of them, but then there was a shout as one of them made a discovery.

"Look at this, Gruck! There's a stick leaning against your windowsill. Could it have escaped that way?"

"How could it reach the windowsill?" objected Gruck. "It didn't have any wings, so it couldn't fly."

"Perhaps it crawled up the wall?"

"But it didn't look like a crawling thing."

"Well, it's certainly not in the room; we've searched every corner of it."

There was a clatter as the stick was thrown away from the window.

"Let's go and look outside! It can't have gotten far."

The door banged. The ogres had left the room.

"I hope they don't discover poor Laughable," whispered Gemma, crawling out of the cushion and taking in great gulps of air. "He's terrified of ogres."

"So am I," shivered Ben-Muzzy. "You heard what he said . . . he's going to pull me to pieces!"

"No, he's not," said Joel. He removed a large feather that had gone down his T-shirt. "We're going to get out of here while they're in the garden."

"How?" said Gemma. "They've taken the gangplank away."

"We couldn't have climbed back up to it, anyhow," pointed out Joel. "We'll have to go through the door."

It was a long drop from the chair to the ground. Fortunately there was a thick woolly rug to break their fall, but for a few moments they sat and gasped and rubbed various parts of their bodies.

"I'm bruised all over," groaned Ben-Muzzy.

They fought their way across the woolly rug. It was like hacking through the jungle. The tufts of rug were thick and matted and taller than they were. They were all exhausted by the time they reached the edge, but they still had another long stretch to go across the carpet. The carpet was soft and squidgy, so that their feet kept sinking into it.

"Like a sort of bog," gasped Gemma.

The ogres had shut the door when they had gone trooping out into the garden, but the twins and Ben-Muzzy were able to crawl underneath it, taking care not to fall through a crack in the floorboards. Once on the other side they found themselves in a vast hall. Faintly, in the far distance, could be seen a second door, with daylight filtering through the glass panels.

"That must be the way out," said Joel.

Gemma drooped. "It's miles away. It'll take us hours."

Even as she spoke, the door opened and three

ogres strode in. One of them was Gruck. His red eyes were glittering with rage, his lips drawn back over his long fangs.

"It must still be in the house," he said. "But don't you worry, I'll find it if it's the last thing I do. And when I find it, I'll pull it to pieces bit by bit!"

Ben-Muzzy and the twins sank back into the shadows. Ben-Muzzy was shaking so much that his knees were knocking together and his teeth were rattling. One of the ogres put his foot down so close to them that Joel could see the thick rim all around the edge of his boot.

The door they had just crawled under was thrown open and then slammed shut. From inside they could hear Gruck throwing the furniture around in his search for Ben-Muzzy.

"We've got to get out of here, quickly!" hissed Joel.

They started off at a run down the hall, but as Gemma had said, it was several miles long and they were soon out of breath.

"What are we going to do?" gasped Ben-Muzzy.

Joel yanked him back into the shadows as the

door opened again. One of the ogres strode back up the passage and out of the front door. They could hear Gruck's voice, shouting angrily.

"I tell you I'll find it if it's the last thing I do! It must still be in the house somewhere!"

And then the other ogre replied, "Well, I can't stay much longer. Whatever it was, it seems to have escaped you."

Gruck gave a loud and terrifying roar of anger. Ben-Muzzy's knees began knocking again.

"Listen," said Joel, "I've an idea." He pulled Gemma and Ben-Muzzy close to him and whispered.

"It's dangerous, but I think it might work . . . when that other ogre comes out, we'll all jump on the rim of his boot and let him carry us down to the front door. Then as soon as he's outside, we can jump off and go back and find Laughable—he's the giant that brought us here," he explained, remembering that Ben-Muzzy had no idea how they had arrived at Gruck's house.

Ben-Muzzy's knees knocked louder than ever. "I don't like it," he muttered.

"Neither do I," said Gemma.

"Well, it's all I can think of," said Joel. "And—Sh!" he added. "He's coming! Get ready to jump!"

In one vast stride, the ogre had reached them. For a second, his enormous boot was only a foot away. Joel made a dive for it, pulling Gemma with him. At the last moment Ben-Muzzy scrambled after them and all three hung there, clinging to a bootlace as thick as a ship's cable, as the ogre banged his way down the passage.

It was a bumpy journey, like riding on a roller coaster. The walls rushed past them at goodness knows how many miles a second; the wind whistled in their ears. At one point Gemma thought she might be sick.

The ogre reached the front door, opened it, and went thumping out. Clump, he went, down the front step. His boot smashed into the ground with such force that the twins and Ben-Muzzy were thrown right off. Like rag dolls they went hurtling through the air.

Joel was flung high up, right over the garden wall into a soft patch of moss on the other side. Gemma landed on top of a dandelion. Poor Ben-Muzzy found himself suspended, dangling in space with his cloak caught on a rose bush.

Joel picked himself up and stared around.

A sudden gust of wind shook the dandelion from side to side. Gemma clung to it in terror as the stalk dipped and swayed and hundreds of tiny parachutes floated off into the air.

"Grab one, grab one!" yelled Joel, jumping up and down on the other side of the wall. He put his hands together to form a trumpet: "GRAB HOLD OF A PARACHUTE!"

Ben-Muzzy, hanging on his rose prickle, heard Joel's suggestion and snatched wildly at a dandelion seed that was drifting past him. In a second he was free of the prickle and was hanging at the end of his parachute, being blown higher and higher by the wind. Gemma watched him for a moment with wide eyes; then she, too, seized hold of a dandelion seed and found herself being carried up into the sky.

Gemma and Ben-Muzzy rose up over the wall and hung for a minute or two above Joel's head. Then a billow of wind caught them and blew them around in circles. The next moment they were being rushed through the air, far away from Joel.

We could be blown for miles! thought
Gemma. Already her arms were aching with the
strain of hanging on. And then, suddenly, she
looked down and saw Laughable, still hiding in
the lane outside Gruck's back garden.

"Help!" shouted Gemma, at the top of her
voice.

The wind dragged her right over Laughable's
head. Gemma closed her eyes and let go, landing
with a thump in his hair. Slowly, Laughable put
up a hand and plucked her out.

"Hello!" he said in surprise. "It's
Joelangemma. Where's the other one of you?
Can we go? Did you rescue your friend that's
going to make me a woolly jersey?"

"He's up there!" yelled Gemma, pointing over
her head.

"Where?" said Laughable.

"There! Up there! Oh, quick, Laughable, you must get him back before he's blown out of sight!"

Ben-Muzzy was a tiny figure up in the clouds, clinging with all his might to the end of his parachute. Laughable stood up, holding Gemma very carefully in one hand. Stretching out the other, he casually plucked Ben-Muzzy out of the air.

"He doesn't look like a twin," he said doubtfully.

"He isn't," said Gemma. "I told you, he's a wizard, and please could you go and get Joel? He's miles away, on the other side of the wall."

Laughable reached Joel in two bounds. He scooped him up from his perch of moss and pushed him into a pocket.

"Hold on tightly," he said. "We're going to run, now, as fast as we can."

Gemma and Ben-Muzzy, crushed together in Laughable's right hand, closed their eyes very tightly. Joel in the back pocket of Laughable's pants, stood on tiptoe and watched the world flash past. He wondered if anyone at school would believe him when he told them he had traveled in a giant's pocket at twice the speed of light.

"We're here," said Laughable, slowing down. "Gruck won't be able to get us now." He sat down on the grass and set the twins and Ben-Muzzy on his knee.

"Thank you very much for helping us," said Gemma politely. She was still feeling a little peculiar inside, from all the dashing around.

"That's all right," said Laughable. "It was very brave of me, because I'm scared of ogres. Can I have my woolly jersey now? A green one," he added anxiously.

"Ah. Yes," said Joel. He looked at Ben-Muzzy. "I hope you've got some magic back, 'cause we promised Laughable you'd make him a woolly jersey if he helped us rescue you. His has got holes all over, and he wants a new one. That should be easy enough, shouldn't it?"

"Well, I don't know," said Ben-Muzzy, doubtfully setting his hat straight. "I've never made a spell for woolly jerseys before. It's usually white rabbits. But I suppose I could try."

"A green one," Gemma reminded him.

"I'll do my best," said Ben-Muzzy. "But I don't

know what shape it'll turn out."

Ben-Muzzy drew his cloak around him and stood up.

"Iggly wiggly werzy," he chanted,
"Make a woolly jersey,
Make it giant-sized and green,
Iggly piggly umpareen."

The twins and Laughable stared around them. There was a puff of smoke and suddenly, from nowhere at all, an enormous woolly cow appeared.

"Yikes!" said Joel.

"What is it?" said Gemma.

Ben-Muzzy looked a little uncomfortable. He cleared his throat a few times.

"It's a cow," he said.

"We can see *that*," said Gemma.

"But we didn't want a cow!" cried Joel. "We wanted a jersey!"

"You know what he's gone and done?" said Gemma. "He made a spell for a jersey and he went and got a Jersey cow instead."

"I did?"

Ben-Muzzy brightened. Until that moment he hadn't known there were such things as Jersey cows. How very clever of him!

"At least its green," he said.

Joel groaned. "You don't *have* green cows."

"And anyway," said Gemma, "how can Laughable wear a cow?"

"You didn't say anything about wearing it." Ben-Muzzy shuffled, defensively. "All you said was a green woolly Jersey, and that's what I've given you. If—"

At this point they were interrupted by a loud rumbling noise and Laughable's knee began to bounce up and down. Gemma looked at him in alarm.

"Ho ho ho!" roared Laughable. He had picked up his woolly cow and was chuckling happily to himself. He seemed to have forgotten the twins and Ben-Muzzy. "Ho ho ho!" he roared, scattering them in all directions as he rose to his feet.

The earth shook as Laughable, still clutching his cow, began leaping up and down.

"I've got something all of my own!" he chanted in delight. "I've got something all of my own, my own, my own."

"Hey, stop it!" shouted Joel. "You're going to

tread on us in a minute!"

Laughable didn't hear him. He gave one extra-terrific leap and bounded out of sight. Ben-Muzzy heaved a sigh of relief.

"Quick!" he said. "Let's get out of here! Join hands—make a magic circle!"

The twins obediently did so. The circle began.

"Six steps to the left," chanted Ben-Muzzy. "Six steps to the right. Then around we go, and around we g—"

Ben-Muzzy broke off. A great cloud had suddenly fallen across the sky. There was a loud flapping of wings and a strange, harsh croaking: *praark, praark, praark*! Ben-Muzzy froze.

"What's the matter?" said Joel.

"Why have we stopped?" asked Gemma.

They looked up.

"It's only a crow," said Joel.

It wasn't a crow. It was a raven. Ben-Muzzy shivered. It was too late to stop the spell now he had started, but with a raven hovering overhead there was no telling what would become of them. Ravens were witches' creatures, and witches dabbled in black magic . . .

Chapter Eight

Almost as soon as Ben-Muzzy had finished reciting his spell a great wind blew up. It came crashing and wailing through the treetops, snapping off twigs and branches, blowing leaves helter-skelter in all directions. Gemma felt it tugging at her clothes, and she cried out in alarm. It seemed almost as if the wind were trying to drag her along with it.

"Hold on!" shouted Joel, but his warning came too late. The wind tore Gemma out of the magic circle and tossed her up into the air.

For a moment Joel stood watching, aghast, as his twin was jerked this way and that, helpless as a blown leaf; then he, too, found himself tugged off his feet and tossed up into the air. All around him was the sound of high-pitched laughter, a shrill shrieking in his ears, as if the wind itself were cackling with glee.

Joel had just time enough to see Ben-Muzzy

also being whirled upwards before a thick blanket of darkness fell over them. It happened quite suddenly, with no warning, as if a light had been switched off. One moment it was daylight, the next moment it was night. The sky was inky black, with no moon and no stars, and the air was full of shrieks and eerie cries.

The wind dropped as suddenly as the darkness had come down. Joel found that he was no longer being blown through the air. He stretched out a cautious hand and felt solid earth beneath him. He stretched out another hand and felt rocks behind him. And then he stretched out both hands together and felt something warm. The something warm gave a frightened squeal.

"G-Gemma?" said Joel.

"J-Joel?" said Gemma.

They hurled themselves at each other.

"I thought I was all alone!" gasped Gemma. "I didn't know what had happened or where we were."

"I don't know what's happened either," said Joel. "But if you ask me, Ben-Muzzy's gone and messed it up again."

"It wasn't my fault!" protested a familiar

voice, somewhere to Joel's right. "Evil got into the magic circle."

Ben-Muzzy came crawling toward them. Gemma could just make out his yellow cloak in the darkness.

"So where are we?" hissed Joel.

"I'm n-not sure, but,"—Ben-Muzzy swallowed—"if we've landed where I think we've landed—"

There was silence.

"What?" said Joel.

"It can't be worse than the ogres," said Gemma. "Can it?"

Before Ben-Muzzy could reply there was a

loud rushing sound over their heads and a long cackle of laughter. Ben-Muzzy fell flat on the ground, pulling the twins with him. For a few moments they lay there, hardly daring to breathe.

"What was it?" whispered Joel, at last. "What was it, making that noise?"

Ben-Muzzy picked himself up and did his best to keep his knees from knocking together. "I rather th-think," he said, "that it was a w-witch."

"A witch?" said Joel. "That's great, that is. That's all we need!"

"Are witches bad?" asked Gemma. "I thought you could get good ones."

"There's no such thing as a good witch," said Ben-Muzzy, and he shook all over from the tips of his shoes to the point of his hat. "That's just a story they tell, to fool people. All witches are bad. They have the same powers as wizards, but wizards use white magic and witches use black."

"I suppose you are *sure* it was a witch?" said Joel. "I mean, we haven't actually seen any witches, have we? I mean, it could have been a—an eagle, or something."

"What about all the d-dreadful noise?" said Gemma. "That c-can't be eagles."

"So maybe we're in the jungle," said Joel. "In the jungle with hyenas and things. Hyenas laugh like that . . . specially at night they laugh like that," he added, but he sounded doubtful.

"There's only one way to find out," said Ben-Muzzy, pulling his cloak around him to give himself courage. "I will go and investigate."

"We'll all go and investigate," said Gemma firmly. "We'll lose each other if we split up."

Dimly, as their eyes grew accustomed to the dark, they were able to make out the line of rocks behind them. It seemed that most of the noise was coming from the far side.

"We'll creep up to the top," said Ben-Muzzy, "and see if we can see anything . . . but whatever you do, don't make a sound!"

They made their way over the rocks as silently as they could, crouching on all fours, close to the ground. Joel was the first to reach the top. He gave a gasp that brought Gemma and Ben-Muzzy hurrying to his side.

"What is it, what is it?" whispered Gemma.

Joel clapped a hand to her mouth. "Sh!"

The rocks formed part of an enormous stone circle. Inside the circle the ground was flat and grassy, and in the center a large cauldron was bubbling and hissing and giving off a curious purple light which hovered in the air. By this light the twins and Ben-Muzzy could see that the circle was filled with hundreds of black-robed figures wearing tall steeple hats. Their hair was long and greasy, their faces thin and cruel, their close-set yellow eyes glittering and winking in the purple light.

Joel gulped once or twice, and then asked, in a voice that was not quite steady: "Are they— witches?"

"Yes," said Ben-Muzzy, hoarsely. "They're witches."

Some of the witches were leaping and dancing around the cauldron, their shrieks and cackles filling the air. Some of them were huddled in groups, their heads close together, their black cloaks spread out like wings. Some seemed to be holding conversations with toads and black cats, some were dancing in private circles of their own, and all the time more and more were pouring in from the air, sitting astride their broomsticks with their black cats perched behind them.

"What are they doing?" whispered Gemma,

urgently. "Why are there so many of them?"

Ben-Muzzy licked his lips. "We must have arrived on their meeting night. Once every year they have a grand meeting, and all the witches in the land gather together and practice black magic and dance around the cauldron until dawn. As soon as the first ray of light appears in the sky, they jump on their broomsticks and fly off in all directions . . . it's what's known as a witch hunt."

"What are they—um—hunting for?" said Gemma.

"Sacrifices. They all take an oath that before sunset they'll provide a sacrifice for the Sacred Plain."

"R-really?" said Joel, as carelessly as he could. "What sort of—um—sacrifice?"

"And what is the Sacred Plain?" said Gemma.

The Sacred Plain, explained Ben-Muzzy, was a deserted stretch of land where nothing lived and nothing grew. It was a dead land, bleached white by the light of the moon, for the sun never rose on the Sacred Plain. It was so vast, said Ben-Muzzy, that not even the witches themselves had explored the whole of it. Some people said it went on forever. And once a year, after the grand meeting, all the witches gathered there at sunset, for just once a year the rays of the dying sun caught the edge of the plain, shooting javelins of fire into the bleached land. It was then that the witches made their sacrifices. The plain, said Ben-Muzzy, was full of statues; and each and every statue had once been a living soul that the witches had turned to stone.

Gemma crouched silent and shocked, but Joel stuck out his lower lip and refused to be impressed.

"No one's going to turn me into a stone!" he announced fiercely.

"If they catch you," said Ben-Muzzy, "there's nothing you can do about it."

"Well, they're not going to catch me!" declared Joel. He hadn't faced up to ogres and been turned into puddles of mud only to fall prey to a bunch of witches. "We obviously have to get away before they start the hunt. Let's creep off while it's still dark and start looking for some oak trees; then soon as you've enough magic back we can move on, quick, before they find us."

Ben-Muzzy shook his head. "Oak trees won't help. Once you're in the Land of the Witches there's only one way to get out, and that's by broomstick. And I doubt if anyone," he said gloomily, "has ever managed to steal a witch's broomstick and get away with it."

"Why not?"

"Because for one thing, not many people know how to deal with broomsticks, and for another thing, no witch ever leaves a broomstick unguarded. There's always a black cat keeping watch."

"Cats are easy enough to deal with," said Joel.

"That's what you think!" said Ben-Muzzy. "I've told you before, black cats are very temperamental animals."

"Well, it's no good just sitting here and waiting to be caught," declared Joel. "We have to get out somehow, and if the only way to go is by broomstick, we'll just have to go by broomstick."

"But we don't know how to use one!" wailed Gemma.

"I do," said Ben-Muzzy unexpectedly. "Apart

from witches, wizards are probably the only people that do. It's one of the things they teach us in school."

"In school?" said Gemma. "What a funny thing to teach!"

"It's one of the classics . . . like Ancient Wizardry and Lost Arts. You have to learn about them, even though they're not used any more."

"Like people doing Latin," Joel broke in impatiently. "The important thing is, Ben-Muzzy knows how to fly broomsticks. At least,"—he looked across at Ben-Muzzy—"he says he does. It's not something that's going to go wrong, is it, like your spells?"

"No," said Ben-Muzzy, humbly. "It's really very simple. All you have to do is talk backward. For instance, if you wanted to tell a broomstick to go west, you'd just say—," Ben-Muzzy concentrated for a moment—"you'd just say 'tsew og' and it would start off in the right direction immediately."

"All right," said Joel. "So all we have to do is find a broomstick, and that shouldn't be too difficult. There must be hundreds of them down there, and I don't know if you've noticed, but there aren't any witches flying around any more. They must all have arrived."

"And how do you think you're going to deal with the black cats?" said Ben-Muzzy. "As soon as they catch sight of us, they'll sound the alarm."

"Well—," Joel frowned and bit his lip. "Well, we could—we could—"

"I know!" said Gemma. "I know what we can do! We can creep around the outside of the circle till we find a broomstick all by itself, without any witch; then Joel can hide behind a rock and make his dog noise. Joel does good dog noises," she told Ben-Muzzy proudly.

"Yes, I do," agreed Joel. "I bet if I make my angry dalmatian noise it'll be enough to scare away a dozen rotten old black cats."

"Let's go and try it immediately," urged Gemma. "We don't know what time it is in this horrible land. It might start getting light at any moment."

"All right." Joel turned and began picking his way carefully back over the rocks. "Before we do it, Ben-Muzzy had better work out what he's going to say. It's not so easy to talk backward and we'll need to make a quick getaway."

"It's no use," said Ben-Muzzy. "You'll never get rid of the black cat."

"You haven't heard his angry dalmatian noise," said Gemma.

Ben-Muzzy sighed. "Well, *if* we get rid of the cat and *if* we manage to steal a broomstick, I will tell it to take us to Wollibar's Cave."

"What's that backward?" demanded Joel.

"Wait a minute," said Ben-Muzzy. "It won't take me a second to work it out. I used to be top of the class for talking backward. Just wait a minute."

"Do you have to put the whole sentence backward, or just each word?' said Gemma.

"Sh!" hissed Joel. "You'll mess him up."

"Evac srabillow" began Ben-Muzzy, slowly, "ot—su—ekat. There! That was pretty quick wasn't it? Evac srabillow ot su ekat. Evac srabillow ot su ekat. You see, you put everything backward. Some people find it quite difficult, but I never had any trouble with it. Why, I remember once—"

"Yes, yes, yes," said Joel hastily. "Never mind

about that now! Let's go and find a broomstick before you forget what you're going to tell it. You'd better keep repeating it to yourself as we go."

They set off along the rocks, keeping well on the outside of the circle, with Ben-Muzzy muttering his sentence to himself. Now and again one of them would slip or dislodge a stone, but by this time the grand meeting of witches was making so much noise that there was no danger of anyone hearing them. The air was full of shrieks and cries as all the witches joined the wild leaping and dancing around the cauldron.

"Over there!" Joel grabbed Gemma's hand and pointed to the far side of the circle. "See? There's one broomstick standing all by itself. That's the one we'll take. Come on!"

They hurried around the circle until they reached the broomstick. A large black cat was curled up by the side of it. Its nose was tucked into its tail, but one green eye was open and glinting through the purple light.

"You see what I mean?" said Ben-Muzzy.

Joel took no notice of him.

"We'll hide behind this rock," he whispered. "As soon as I have the cat out of the way we'll leap onto the broomstick.

"OK," said Gemma.

Ben-Muzzy just shrugged a shoulder.

Joel crouched down behind a rock, made his hands into a trumpet around his mouth, and gave a low growl. The cat pricked an ear. Joel growled again, a little louder this time. Then he gave a deep, threatening bark. The cat sprang to its feet, its tail waving and all its hair on end.

"Grr-uff! Grrr-rrr-uff!" went Joel.

Gemma chewed anxiously at her thumbnail. Ben-Muzzy repeated his sentence over and over. Joel snarled and growled. The cat began slowly to back away, spitting and hissing.

"Grr-uff! Rrr-uff, rr-uff-uff-uff!" went Joel again.

The cat gave a loud yowl. It turned and ran off, straight into the circle of leaping witches.

"Quick!" yelled Joel.

He made a dash for the broomstick, followed by Gemma and Ben-Muzzy. All three of them leaped onto it and Ben-Muzzy grasped it firmly by the handle.

"Evac srabillow—," he began. He stopped.

"Go on! Go on!" said Joel, prodding Ben-Muzzy in the ribs.

"What's the matter?" said Gemma.

"I've forgotten it! I've forgotten the sentence!" Ben-Muzzy clasped a hand to his forehead. "Evac srabillow—srabillow—"

"Hurry!" gasped Gemma, who was staring back over her shoulder. "I think someone's noticed the cat!"

"Evac srabillow—ot su ekat!" said Ben-Muzzy, in a rush. "Hold tight! We're off!"

The broomstick rose into the air. Ben-Muzzy was holding on to the handle, Joel was holding on to Ben-Muzzy, Gemma was holding on to Joel.

"Faster, faster!" she told Ben-Muzzy.

"It can't go any faster," said Ben-Muzzy. "It's only meant for one person. Three's too heavy for it."

"But they've seen us! They'll come after us!"

The twins were staring down at the circle of witches. Hundreds of yellow eyes were glinting up at them, the air was full of dreadful screams and curses, the magic cauldron splittered and heaved.

Ben-Muzzy also stared down. He laughed, and waved a hand. The witches shook their fists angrily.

"It's OK," he told the twins. "Once they've started their grand meeting they can't fly away from it till dawn. Now that we're in the air, we're all right. There's not a thing they can do about it. This time," said Ben-Muzzy joyfully, "we really are going home!"

Chapter Nine

The broomstick flew on through the darkness. At first Gemma had been scared of losing her balance and falling off, but Ben-Muzzy explained to her that once you were actually traveling on a broomstick, it was not possible to fall off.

"I wonder if it would be the same on an ordinary broom?" said Gemma.

"Certainly not!" Ben-Muzzy was indignant. The very idea! Trying to ride on an ordinary broom! He hoped Gemma wasn't starting to think that magic was easy. "Not every broomstick can fly," he said. "Just as not everyone can cast spells," he added.

"Oh, absolutely not," agreed Gemma.

The first faint light of dawn was beginning to seep into the sky, sending out exploratory fingers through the darkness.

"Not much farther to go now," said Ben-

Muzzy, bouncing up and down and making Gemma feel sick. "I can recognize the scenery."

"I'm beginning to feel at home on a broomstick," said Joel, staring down over the side. "I'll be quite sorry to get off."

They flew on through the pink morning, into the rays of the rising sun, until suddenly Ben-Muzzy gave an excited shout and the broomstick tipped itself nose-to-the-ground and began to dive down toward the earth.

"We're here!" yelled Ben-Muzzy. "We're back! Look! There's Wollibar's cave!"

The broomstick settled itself gently onto a patch of grass outside. A notice over the entrance said:

G. H. W. Wollibar
Cat parking at rear

"I wonder what G. H. W. stands for?" whispered Gemma. "George Henry William?"

"Grand High Wizard," whispered Joel.

The twins stared into the cave. A large magic cauldron, bright and shining, stood in the center of it. A small wizard wearing a green cloak was busy polishing it. Nearby, a black cat was sitting washing itself.

Ben-Muzzy stepped up importantly to the entrance of the cave. He cleared his throat a few times and coughed. The small wizard in the green cloak looked up. He had pale blue eyes the size of saucers, and they grew in astonishment to the size of soup plates as he saw Ben-Muzzy.

"You're back!" he gasped.

"Yes, I'm back," said Ben-Muzzy carelessly. He turned to the twins. "This is Podnock," he said. "Podnock, these are two friends of mine. They're twins."

"Hello," said the twins.

Podnock stood and gaped.

"We came by broomstick," said Ben-Muzzy, even more carelessly than before. "I've parked it just outside. I hope that's all right?"

"Of course," said Podnock. And then he

dropped his polishing rag and said, "*Broom*stick?"

"We picked it up in the Land of Witches," said Ben-Muzzy.

Podnock's eyes widened to the size of two big trash can lids. He turned and darted through one of the doors at the back of the cave. The twins could hear his voice, shrill with excitement: "Ben-Muzzy's come back, Ben-Muzzy's come back! He's been to the Land of Witches and he's come on a broomstick, and he's brought some twins with him!"

And then another voice, deep and gruff, said, "Great magic cauldrons!" and the Grand High Wizard himself came into the cave.

Wollibar was a very Grand High Wizard indeed. He wore a crimson hat decorated with silver stars, and a crimson cloak with a silver band around the edges. He had a long white beard and he carried a silver wand.

He looked at Ben-Muzzy and he said, "So you've come back, have you?" and he looked at the twins and he said, "So you're twins, are you?"

"Yes," said Ben-Muzzy and the twins

at the same time.

"Bless my soul!" said Wollibar, shaking his beard. "Bless my magic stars, I never did in all my life!"

"We've been all over the place," said Ben-Muzzy importantly. "We've been to Wishing Land and Giant Land—"

"And Joel got turned into a puddle of mud—"

"And Ben-Muzzy was captured by an ogre—"

"And—"

"Don't all talk at once!" said Wollibar, raising his magic wand. He looked severely at Ben-Muzzy. "I've been up all night searching through my spell books for a spell to get you back again. All the Grand High Wizards in the land have been called in to help. It's been most inconvenient. Many of them were in the middle of extremely important spells when you disappeared."

"I'm very sorry," said Ben-Muzzy, hanging his head.

"I don't know about being sorry," said Wollibar. "I think we'd better go right off to the Grand Order and let them know that you're back. Where's this broomstick of yours? We might as well use it, now that it's here."

They walked out of the cave and stared at the broomstick.

"Remarkable!" said Wollibar. "Quite remarkable! I've never seen a broomstick in full working order before. The ones in our museums are centuries old."

He examined it from top to bottom, then turned to Ben-Muzzy. "Well, come along, come along!" he ordered. "Don't just stand around staring. You don't seem to realize the trouble you've caused. The sooner we let them know you're back, the better it will be for everybody."

"What about us?" said Joel anxiously. "We've got to get home pretty quickly. We promised our mother we'd be back for dinner."

"And I promised you'd help them," added Ben-Muzzy, mounting the broomstick behind Wollibar.

Wollibar waved his wand. "You'd better come along to the Grand Order and we'll see what we can do."

The twins scrambled onto the broomstick behind Ben-Muzzy. Podnock stood wistfully watching.

"I suppose I couldn't come too?" he asked.

"Broomsticks are not built to carry all this crowd of people!" snapped Wollibar. He poked impatiently at Podnock with his wand. "Get on, get on, and hurry up about it!"

Hastily, Podnock climbed onto the broomstick behind the twins. At the last moment the black cat strolled over and climbed solemnly onto Wollibar's shoulder.

"All aboard?" said Wollibar. "Right, let's go. Redro dnarg eht ot og ew ffo!"

"What was all that?" whispered Gemma in Ben-Muzzy's ear, as the broomstick rose rather uncertainly off the ground.

Ben-Muzzy muttered the words to himself a few times, then turned back to Gemma. "Off we go to the Grand Order," he translated.

"Wollibar's good at talking backward, isn't he?" said Gemma admiringly.

"He's older than I am," said Ben-Muzzy, with a sniff.

The broomstick took them right to the steps of the front entrance of the Grand Order. Ben-Muzzy could hardly believe it was only yesterday that he had taken his examination and disappeared. He wondered if he was still a second-class wizard or if they had made him a first-class while he was away.

Wollibar led the way through the building and up to the Master Wizard's room, with the black cat and Ben-Muzzy, the twins and Podnock following at his heels. The Master Wizard was in conference with several Grand High Wizards. Ben-Muzzy recognized one of them: It was the one whose hat he had knocked off when he had been practicing flying.

"I knew something like this would happen sooner or later," he was saying. "Why, only yesterday the young scoundrel came flying through a door and knocked me over. He upset my cat and he ruined my hat and—"

"So you said before," remarked the Master Wizard, rather wearily. "The question is—" He caught sight of Wollibar, and bowed to him. "Good afternoon, Grand High. No news of him yet, I suppose?"

And then he caught sight of Ben-Muzzy, and then he caught sight of the twins, and his mouth fell open. He pushed back his chair and staggered to his feet.

"Bless my magic buttons!" he gasped. "Great black cats and shining cauldrons! He's come back!"

"By broomstick!" burst out Podnock, who was in a state of high excitement after his ride. "He's been everywhere! He's been to the Land of Witches—"

"And the Land of Giants—"

"And Joel got turned into a puddle of mud—"

"And Ben-Muzzy made himself invisible—"

"And please, I'm very sorry for all the trouble I've caused," said Ben-Muzzy, "and did I pass my examination?"

All the Grand High Wizards laughed except

the one whose hat had been knocked off when Ben-Muzzy was flying. He said, "Bless my toenails, what are these young wizards coming to?" and stalked out of the room.

"I think," said Gemma, "that Ben-Muzzy should pass 'cause he's done an awful lot of good magic while he's been away."

"Who is this?" asked the Master Wizard, staring very hard at Gemma.

"She's a twin," said Ben-Muzzy. "And that's another twin. They've been helping me. I couldn't have gotten back without them."

"And the twin thinks you deserve to pass your exam, does she?"

"Yes," said Gemma firmly. "We think Ben-Muzzy's a very good wizard."

"Except," remembered Joel, "when he magics pink elephants instead of dogs."

Gemma glared at him, and Ben-Muzzy grew as pink as the elephant had been.

"What's all this about dogs?" asked the Master Wizard.

"I couldn't help it," said Ben-Muzzy, earnestly. "I'd never done a spell for dogs before. I'm all right at white rabbits, I can get them white all over, but dogs are difficult."

"Might one inquire why you were attempting dogs in the first place?" said the Master.

"It was for us," said Gemma. "He promised—well." She bit her lip.

"I promised," said Ben-Muzzy, "that if the twins helped me get back I'd magic up a dog for them."

"And they have helped you get back," said Wollibar. "So where is the dog?"

Everyone in the room turned to look at Ben-Muzzy. Joel felt sorry that he had ever mentioned it.

"It's all right," he said. "It doesn't really matter. We'll get one for our birthday if we wait long enough."

"No, no, no!" said the Master. "A dog you were promised, and a dog you shall have. And if second-class junior wizard Ben-Muzzy can manage to produce one for you, I will make him a first-class junior on the spot."

Ben-Muzzy turned slowly scarlet with pride.

"You haven't done it yet," warned Podnock. "You'd better not make any more of your silly mistakes."

Gemma tugged at Ben-Muzzy's sleeve. "It's not important what kind of dog," she whispered. "Just any dog will do, as long as it passes your exam for you."

"Thank you," said Ben-Muzzy gratefully.

He stared around the room at all the assembled Grand High Wizards, and he couldn't help trembling just a little bit. Imagine having to do a spell in front of six Grand Highs and one Master and Wollibar himself, not to mention Podnock, who was bound to split his sides laughing if anything went wrong.

"Can I go and do it in a corner?" asked Ben-Muzzy shyly.

"Do it anywhere you like!" said the Master. "We'll turn our backs if it will make thinking easier."

"Yes, it will," said Ben-Muzzy, earnestly nodding his head.

The six Grand Highs, the Master, and Wollibar gravely turned their backs on Ben-Muzzy. Only Podnock and the twins were watching him.

Podnock was thinking, I bet he does something silly, and Joel was thinking, I hope it's a dalmatian, and Gemma was thinking, I hope nothing goes wrong for him.

All three watched anxiously as Ben-Muzzy placed himself in one corner of the room. He muttered a few words to himself, made a few magic passes, and a shiny black top hat appeared in his hand. Gemma breathed a sigh of relief: The first part of the spell had worked all right!

Anyone can produce top hats, thought Podnock, to himself. It's the dog that's difficult.

Ben-Muzzy closed his eyes and concentrated very hard. He had a picture of a dog in mind. It was black and white and shaggy with hair all over its eyes.

"Fillivan fullivan upwigo!"

The hat flew up into the air. Clouds of smoke filled the room. As they disappeared, the twins could see that there was a small bundle of fur at Ben-Muzzy's feet. Podnock stared at it very hard. The six Grand Highs, the Master, and Wollibar all turned around, and they also stared very hard.

The small bundle sat up and shook itself and gave an uncertain whimper. It was white, with black spots all over it. It had a very long body and very short legs and very long hair. A fringe grew over its eyes. Its nose was pink, its tail was curly. One ear was droopy, the other was cocked. It was like no other dog the twins had ever seen, but it was, undoubtedly, a dog.

"You've done it!" cried Gemma joyfully.

"Is it all right?" asked Ben-Muzzy, with an anxious look at it.

"What is it?" demanded Podnock.

"That is what I would like to know," agreed the Master.

Gemma rushed across the room and scooped the small bundle into her arms. "It's a puppy!" she said. "The most beautiful puppy!"

The puppy licked her face gratefully.

"I'm going to call her Flossie!"

"Spot!" snapped Joel.

"Flossie!"

"Spot!"

There was a short silence, while the twins stood and glared at each other.

"Why don't you call it Primple?" suggested Podnock.

The twins turned to look at him.

"What a very good idea!" said Gemma.

"Why ever didn't we think of it before?" said Joel.

"Primple!" they agreed.

"What about me?" asked Ben-Muzzy in a small anxious voice. "I know it's not any special kind of dog, but it is a dog, isn't it?"

"One has to assume so," said the Master, and all the six Grand Highs laughed. Even Wollibar permitted himself a faint smile. And then, when the laughter had died away, the Master stretched out his hand and produced a beautiful green cloak out of the air.

"There you are," he said, holding it out to Ben-Muzzy. "First-class junior wizard, Ben-Muzzy!"

It was the proudest day of Ben-Muzzy's life. Everyone shook hands with him, Joel and Podnock clapped him on the back, Gemma kissed him, and Primple licked his nose.

"There! You've done it!" said Joel, triumphantly. "And now you'll be a Grand High Wizard in no time!"

"Oh, no," said Ben-Muzzy, looking shocked. "It takes years and years and years to become a

Grand High."

"But I'm sure you will be one, one day," said Gemma. "And now, if you don't mind, I really think we should be going."

"Because of not missing dinner," said Joel.

"And thank you very much for Primple—"

"And for the ride on the broomstick. Graham Roberts isn't ever going to believe it!"

"Talking of broomsticks," said Wollibar, "I think that's probably the quickest way of sending you home. I'll tell it to bring itself back here again as soon as you've arrived. How does that idea strike you?"

The idea struck the twins as being very good indeed. They followed Wollibar downstairs, and Ben-Muzzy and Podnock, and the Master Wizard and the six Grand High Wizards and the black cat all followed behind.

"On you get," said Wollibar.

The twins climbed aboard the broomstick, with Joel in front and Gemma sitting behind with Primple in her arms.

"I'm going to miss you," said Ben-Muzzy, looking forlorn in spite of his new green cloak.

"We're going to miss you, too," agreed

Gemma, who looked just as forlorn.

"But now he's got the broomstick," pointed out Joel, "he can come and visit us whenever he wants."

"So he can!" said Gemma, cheering up.

"So I can!" echoed Ben-Muzzy. "As soon as I have my vacation, I'll come and see you again!"

"Perhaps we can do some more exploring?" said Joel, hopefully, but already the broomstick was rising into the air as Wollibar said the magic words "Ereh kcab emoc neht rennid rof emoh sniwt eht ekat!"

"Yikes!" said Joel. "I hope he's sent us in the right direction!"

The broomstick landed gently in the middle of Three Penny Woods. The twins climbed off and stared around with wide eyes.

"We're back!" said Joel. "I can't believe it . . . I can't believe any of it really happened." He rubbed his eyes. "Did it happen?" he said. "Or have I been dreaming? Pinch me and see if I'm awake!"

"Of course you're awake!" said Gemma. "The broomstick's still here, isn't it? And Primple's still here, isn't he?"

Primple barked loudly to prove that he was, and the broomstick, remembering Wollibar's instructions, slowly rose into the air and disappeared through the clouds.

"You see?" said Gemma.

Somewhere in the distance, a church clock struck the hour. Primple put his head on one side, and the twins stood and listened.

One—two—three—four—five—six—

"Six o'clock!" said Gemma.

"Time for dinner!" said Joel. "Come on!"

THE END